FROM THE CLUTCHES OF EVIL

A *Jillian Bradley* Mystery

Nancy Jill Thames

This is a work of fiction. Names, characters, places and incidents either are the product of the author's imagination or are used fictitiously, and any resemblance to actual persons, living or dead, business establishments, events, or locales is entirely coincidental or used with permission. *NJT*

Cover photo: *Andre Govia*
Author Photo: *Glamour Shots Barton Creek*
Yorkshire terrier: *"Romeo"* Courtesy: *Dan & Sara Olla*

ISBN-13: 978-1453822609
ISBN-10: 1453822607
Category: *Fiction/Mystery & Detective/Women Sleuths*

TO MY HUSBAND

For his helpful criticism and loving support

FROM THE CLUTCHES OF EVIL

The Righteous One takes note of the house of the wicked
and brings the wicked to ruin.

Proverbs 20:12 NIV

1

Madison looked nervously toward the back of the house, hoping and praying that no one would see them. Satisfied that they were still safe, she looked at the young man, so handsome with his neatly cropped auburn hair and soft brown eyes.

She knew he was vulnerable.

"Listen to me," she said. "We've got to get out! If we don't go right now we may never have another chance."

He looked at Madison, her long blond hair whipping back and forth as she looked at the house, and then at him. Her angel face and green eyes had captured his heart, and he knew he would do whatever she wanted.

He did not comprehend danger, and yet he could sense that her instincts were right.

"All right, I'm coming," he said. "But you have to tell me why we have to leave like this without telling anyone."

Madison's heart began to beat faster as she motioned

for him to be quiet.

He followed her, and together they walked quickly to the end of the long garage and raised the garage door.

The car was still there.

She bent down and checked the back tire. The dry leaf she had placed in front of the tire a week before lay undisturbed. The car had not been driven.

As she stood up, she thought about the terrible risk she was about to take, and a chill ran down her spine.

She looked into his questioning eyes.

"You just have to trust me," she said.

Madison pulled the tarp off the small compact, opened the door, and got in the driver's seat.

"Come on! Get in the car."

She knew the keys were still in the ignition because it was in the plan. She had checked the car out with a flashlight the week before after she had seen what had been going on.

"Don't think about that now," she told herself. "Just get him away from here."

Madison unlocked the passenger door from the inside, and the young man got in, fastening his seatbelt.

"Are you sure you know what you're doing, Madison? It's going to be dark soon."

"Just hang on!" she said, starting the ignition.

She pulled out slowly from the garage, heading for the road she had discovered that ran behind the property.

The road led back down the hill. Up until two weeks ago, she never knew it existed.

Madison anxiously glanced in her left side mirror to check the house one last time. When she saw the two men coming out through the back door, she felt fear gripping her once again.

When the men saw the couple racing away, the older man yelled at them.

"Hey, stop! Where do you think you're going?"

Madison floored the accelerator and drove away, down the winding narrow road, not bothering to look back.

The men wasted no time.

"Madison, they're following us. What's wrong? You're scaring me! What have you done? We can't do this. You need to stop right now. I'll tell them something so you won't get in trouble, just take me back."

"No, I can't—you don't understand. You can't go back there," she said, looking furtively in the rear view mirror to see how close behind they were.

The men gained on the fleeing couple, and both cars sped up.

When the road ended at the back of the old feed barn, Madison knew exactly where she was. She could see that Main Street was only a block away and drove down an alley that she knew would take her right to it.

She made a left on Main Street, taking her through the outskirts of the small town, and then made a right turn onto Benito Canyon Road, a long winding stretch bordered on one side with oak forests and thick undergrowth, and on the other, a deep narrow gorge that held the creek bed.

The gorge was filled with a heavy undergrowth of wild grasses and trees lining the banks of the slowly trickling creek. Willows, buckeyes, and sycamores were home to wild turkeys and deer—hawks made their homes in the branches. The creek provided necessary water for all of their existence.

The deer usually waited until dusk when they felt safe before venturing from their hidden shelters to feed, but on occasion, hunger made them venture out earlier in the afternoon.

A doe, followed by her young fawn, spotted a particular favorite grass to nibble across the road on the hill above the gorge.

The deer stepped onto the road just as Madison glanced

in her rear view mirror, checking the car in pursuit. The young man turned to look as well.

The men were gaining fast.

Neither saw the deer as they started to cross, and before she could swerve to miss it, in a split second, Madison's car struck the doe, killing it instantly as the frightened fawn ran back into the undergrowth.

The couple screamed as their car flew into the air, turning over several times and then careening into the gorge, rolling over and over, until it finally came to rest in front of a large boulder.

The young man opened his eyes and saw Madison slumped over the steering wheel, blood trickling from her face, her body grotesquely contorted.

He glanced up to where their car had gone off the road and saw the two men pull up. Both men got out and looked down at the crash.

Suddenly, they turned and got back in the car, and then drove away. He wondered why they left him there to die.

Then, there was only blackness.

❧2❧

"My hair will just have to do, I suppose," I reasoned, taking a last look in the entryway mirror and turning on the front porch light.

"Come on, Teddy," I called to my Yorkie. "Let's go get in the car!"

Teddy walked slowly to where I was standing and stretched from a late afternoon nap. He looked at me as if to say, "Where are we off to, Mistress?"

"We're going over to LaBelle's Nursery in Canyon Grove to discuss the rose workshop I'm doing in January. Verity can never make up her mind about what it should include due to the countless questions she gets each year. This was the only time we could get together, even though it *is* right before the party. We're supposed to be there in twenty minutes, so let's get going!"

I put his red rhinestone studded collar and leash on the front seat of my beautiful, brand-new, white Jeep Cherokee, and Teddy climbed onto the back seat, lying down like the good dog he was.

I loved driving my new car. I had become a loyal Jeep fan after my old one had served me faithfully for ten years, but I knew it was worn out, and it was time I bought a new one. I was grateful for the new syndications of my column that had allowed me to replace my trusted old friend.

"This won't take too long. I already have an idea of what I'm going to include. I could write a *book* on roses — just from answering all the questions readers have sent me. We'll still have time to get back and get ready, I think," I said to Teddy, glad to have him for a listening companion since I lived alone.

I enjoy driving over to Canyon Grove because it always takes me out of busy traffic I so often encounter, and I love passing though the bucolic countryside filled with centuries old trees, whose branches often overhang the road.

Since it was winter, the woods were bare, here and there, with the deciduous trees having shed their leaves. The canopied oaks, however, remained leafed out, with their small, grayish-green leaves clinging to sprawling branches.

After passing under the railway bridge, I traveled down the access road without seeing another car for several miles, glancing occasionally at the ancient trees dotting the sun drenched golden hills, until I turned onto Benito Canyon Road, which eventually led into the small community of Canyon Grove.

Before I reached the turnoff to LaBelle's, a small older model car sped from the small town, ran the stop sign, and turned right.

Another car, following close behind, ran the stop sign as well, and then turned to follow the speeding car. Teddy yipped when he heard the squeal of their tires and jumped into the front seat and into my lap. He began barking furiously.

"You think I should follow them, Teddy?" I asked, somehow needing affirmation that I needed to get involved. Teddy yipped twice in the affirmative, and I began to follow the second car as closely as I dared, without being too obvious.

I didn't see the cause of the crash. I only assumed the driver had lost control, and I watched helplessly as the first car flew into the air, turning over several times, and then careened into the gorge, landing with the horrible sounds of metal crashing against rocks and trees as it rolled over and over before coming to a standstill.

The driver of the second car pulled over to the ledge, and along with his passenger, got out and peered over at the crash. Teddy growled and gave me a look that told me I should get a license plate number, just in case.

I started to slow down, reaching inside my purse and feeling around for a pen and the small notebook I always carry.

I was only a few car lengths behind when the men took one look at me getting ready to pull over, got back into their car, and drove off.

It was too late for me to write down anything, and I knew there were people down there that might need help.

I phoned 911 and told the police what had happened. They pinpointed my location immediately and said they would send a highway patrol officer to help right away, but I couldn't wait.

I opened my door, and Teddy jumped out of the car before I could grab him, and headed down the ravine.

"Teddy, wait!" I cried.

He ran ahead, as if he knew someone's life depended on him. I ran, too, aware that he sensed impending danger.

He looked back, and barked for me to follow him.

I was no match for Teddy's ability to maneuver down the ravine. I followed the path he chose, stepping carefully between the shrubs and trees, flattened by the car as it rolled over them, striking the ground.

I could hear Teddy's barking and followed the sound until I could see him through the dust filling the air and covering the crumpled car.

I stopped cold.

The car had landed on its right side, with the driver hanging precariously over the steering wheel. She was covered in blood, and I couldn't tell whether she was still alive or not. A young man lay unconscious next to the car. It looked as if he had been thrown through a back window. His arms were cut and bleeding from the broken glass.

I silently prayed for God to save him, and the girl, too, although she looked like she wasn't going to make it.

I stooped beside the prostrate figure of the young man, and could tell that he was still breathing. Teddy barked, and I immediately smelled gas coming from the car.

I had to try to save the girl. With all the strength I could muster, I pulled the young man as far away from the car as I could and ordered Teddy to stay with him. Teddy obeyed, and I ran to the car. I was going to climb up and try to open her door when I heard someone yelling and coming down the hill.

"We're coming! Hold on lady!" The highway patrol officers had finally arrived.

"I think the car is going to explode!" I yelled. "Please hurry!"

Three officers ran to the car and managed to get the door open, then deftly extracted the limp form away from the steering wheel.

"Everyone down, now!" the officer in charge shouted.

I grabbed Teddy and placed my body over the young

man to shield him. I closed my eyes and prayed again for God to protect us. Suddenly, the car exploded with a horrific blast, sending burning pieces of metal and shards of glass into the air, raining down on all of us. The cloud of smoke was so heavy that I could barely breathe. When it was finally safe to move, I commanded Teddy to stay with the boy.

I could see a crumpled heap lying next to a burning tree. The girl had literally been blasted out of the officer's arms as the car exploded.

The officer ran to where she lay and gently rolled the girl over on her back, and felt for a pulse. He indicated that there was a faint beat. I silently thanked God and sat beside the girl, holding her head in my lap.

Sirens whirled through the air at the top of the ravine, and more help began to arrive. Firefighters scurried down the steep hill and began spraying chemicals on the burning car and brush that had caught fire. Paramedics arrived with stretchers and followed closely behind. Teddy barked as the boy began to move, and I continued to hold the girl in my arms.

Paramedics motioned for me to let them take over, so I gently rested the girl's bleeding head on the ground, stood up and stepped back. After briefly examining her, they quickly placed the girl on a gurney. I could tell she was badly hurt. The boy sat up, apparently gaining consciousness. He looked dazed and disoriented. I went over to where Teddy was standing guard beside him and asked if he was all right.

"Where am I?" he asked in the voice of a man, coming from the face of a child.

"You and your girlfriend have been in a car accident," I explained. "You're very lucky to be alive."

I helped him to his feet.

"Girlfriend? I don't know what you mean," he said.

"You were with a girl—she was driving the car when you crashed. You may be in shock, so let's just get you out of here," I said.

The police, and a few people who had stopped to help, began to assist us back up to the road, a younger woman carrying Teddy for me.

"Thanks so much for stopping," I told her.

I remembered the men who had left the scene of the accident and knew they were involved somehow, but I didn't have time to think about that right now. I had to see to this boy and make sure he found his way home.

After an arduously long climb, we finally reached the road, and after the ambulance had taken the girl to the hospital, the police began to ask questions.

The officer in charge took out an accident form and asked the boy his name.

"I don't know," he said, still confused from the shock.

The officer proceeded. "Can you tell us what happened?"

The boy stood there, looking at the ground.

"I really can't remember."

The officer looked at me and then back at the boy.

"Young man, do you have any injuries you wish to report? The paramedics examined you and there are no broken bones. You've suffered a bump on the back of your head and a few minor cuts on your arms, but there's nothing that indicates the need to go to the hospital right now, unless you feel the need."

"Officer, why don't we try and get in touch with the boy's parents before he makes a decision like that," I suggested, helpfully.

"All right, son," the officer agreed, "What's your parents' number—I'll call them right now for you so we can get you taken care of."

"I can't tell you, sir. I can't even remember who they are," he said, looking at me blankly.

I knew he must feel terribly lost and decided to take the matter in hand.

"Officer, if you've no objection, I'll take responsibility for him and make sure he gets medical attention until we can find his parents."

A tow truck arrived to haul away what was left of the wreckage. The driver got out and hailed the officer, indicating that he needed to get started. I knew it would be a feat to retrieve such a huge mess of hot debris, and I felt sorry for the men who had to do it.

"Well, ma'am," the officer said, looking at the driver, "I suppose it will be all right if you'll just give me your information so we can contact you for follow up," he said.

I took a business card from my purse and wrote down the date and time of the accident. The officer thanked me for being a good citizen and walked over to speak to the tow truck driver, while I put Teddy and the young man into my car. The officer returned to the three of us, and I handed him my card.

He looked at the card briefly and noted my name.

"Thanks, Mrs. Bradley. Hey—I know who you are! Gee, it's an honor to meet you ma'am," he said, shaking my hand. "I'm a bit of a gardener myself, and I read your column all the time!"

"It's always a pleasure to meet one of my readers. Now officer, don't worry, I'll take very good care of this young man until he gets oriented again." We shook hands again, and he excused himself to file the accident report.

I looked at the disheveled boy and said, "Looks like you're coming home with Teddy and me. By the way, I'm Jillian Bradley. Still don't remember your name?" I asked.

He looked at me and shook his head slowly from side to side.

"It's quite all right," I assured him. "If you did have a name, what would you like it to be?"

"I guess you could call me Luke," he said. "Can we go now? I think I need to lie down."

"Come on," I said, "let's go home."

I put Teddy in the back seat and helped Luke into the front seat, making sure he put his seat belt on.

I didn't try probing into the boy's life. I knew he needed rest and quiet if he was ever going to remember anything.

After a few minutes of silence, he looked out his window and simply stared at the cars going by. I knew he must still be in shock. After we reached home, I pulled the car into the garage and helped him into the house.

"The guest room is upstairs," I said. "Do you feel like climbing them right now?"

"I guess so. I just want to lie down."

"I'll help you get settled," I said kindly.

I helped him up the stairs and into the guest room that I always keep ready. I helped him off with his dirty shoes and socks, turned back the duvet and sheets, and told him he could take off his clothes after I'd stepped out.

"Luke, I'll need to make a call, but Teddy can stay with you if you want. Would you like that?"

"Yes, I would. Thanks…."

"It's all right—you can call me Jillian."

"Thank you, Jillian."

I took a towel from the guest bath adjoining Luke's room, placed it at the foot of his bed, and put Teddy on it.

"I'll clean him up in a minute after I make my call. You rest now. You can clean up whenever you feel like it. I need to get Teddy a bowl of water. Can I bring you a cup of tea and some cookies?"

"Why are you being so nice to me?" was his answer.

"Luke, I try and put myself in the other person's shoes and think about how I would want to be treated if I was having trouble of some kind. When I knew you couldn't even remember your name, I had to help you. If it were me, I hope someone would help me in the same way. It's really pretty simple. Now, would you like a cup of tea? I think it would make you feel better."

"Okay. I'll take the cookies, too, please."

"I'll bring them up as soon as I can. You get comfortable, and I'll be right back," I said, placing Teddy on the towel.

"Stay with Luke, Teddy," I commanded.

Teddy lay down and did as he was told.

I looked at the clock to check the time. Only an hour and a half before my guests arrived! Running down the stairs, I caught a look at myself in the mirror. What a sight! My clothes were covered in dust, and my face was smudged everywhere with dirt.

I went to the kitchen, washed my hands, and started the tea. Now to call Dr. Peters—I made an appointment for him to examine Luke in the morning and requested an in-home nurse to come and stay with Luke overnight. I felt uneasy about his safety knowing those two men might wish to do him harm. I also would feel more comfortable with someone else staying in the house, for appearance sake.

I quickly put some chocolate chip cookies I had just baked on a plate and placed it on a bed tray, along with a napkin, spoon, sugar bowl, small pitcher of milk, and a bowl of fresh water for Teddy. The microwave dinged, indicating the tea was ready. I put the mug on the tray and raced up the stairs as quickly as I could without spilling everything. "Luke, I have your tea ready, may I come in?"

"Sure," he said.

I opened the door, balancing the tray with one hand. Teddy was still lying on his towel being obedient.

"Here's your tea," I said, placing the tray on his lap.

"Teddy, you may get down and have a drink of water."

I placed the bowl on the bathroom floor. Teddy jumped down, went to his bowl, and lapped thirstily.

Luke picked up his cup with long slender fingers, and took a sip of tea.

"This is good. Thank you, Jillian."

"You're very welcome. Listen, I apologize for being in such a hurry, Luke, but I'm having a party here tonight, so I need to get ready. There's a bell in that drawer next to your bed. I'll leave your door open, and if you should need me, just ring it. I have to take a shower now, and I'll be using the hair dryer, so I may not hear you if you ring it right away, but I'll be listening for you. After your tea, you should try to rest. I've ordered a nurse to stay with you until we're sure you're all right. I'll bring you a robe to have handy when you feel like taking a shower. I'll get some more clothes for you in the morning. Is there anything I can get you before I leave?"

"No, thank you. And thank you for helping me. I could be dead right now if you hadn't."

"Everything is going to be all right," I said. "Get some rest, and I'll check on you after I get ready."

I put Teddy back on the towel and told him to stay. When I brought the robe to Luke, he smiled for the first time.

❧3❧

I got ready for my party as quickly as I could, knowing that I had done it before in just forty-five minutes flat. I just had to be ready on time tonight—it was too important of an occasion.

I was glad I had laid out my outfit before I left to go to LaBelle's—an elegant, floor-length black gown, with capped sleeves and touches of gold thread running through the fabric. The caterers would be here any minute. LaBelle's! I had forgotten all about the appointment. I grabbed my cell and left a quick message of apology, briefly explaining the crash. I sprayed my hair with a quick sprits of hairspray, stepped out of my slippers and into my flats, took one last look in the mirror and voila! I was all set. The back doorbell rang, and I rushed to the kitchen, being careful not to trip in my long gown.

"Come in," I said, opening the door.

The caterers began bringing in the food and serving paraphernalia. I glanced outside and looked for any signs of the men I had seen leaving the crash site. I would recognize them by their heights and hair if I ever saw them again. Not seeing anyone, I closed the door and prepared to greet my guests.

I had decided to give an intimate dinner party to announce the engagement of two dear friends of mine. Cecilia Chastain was my personal assistant from time to time, taking care of Teddy on business trips when I needed her. She was like a daughter to me. *The Clover Hills Daily* had recently hired her as a part time news writer. Her fiancé, Walter Montoya, Jr. was a fine young man whom I first met when he was a valet for The Ritz-Carlton Hotel in Half Moon Bay. Cecilia had been a housekeeper at the hotel when we all met. He was now working in the Clover Hills Police Department as a brand new detective.

Sadly, Cecilia's mother had passed away only a few months ago from an aneurism. Cecilia was devastated to lose her mother so early, and I felt giving the engagement party was the only thing to do, knowing the pain and heartache she and her father were experiencing. There would be sixteen of us. Just the closest of friends would be attending. I went upstairs to look in on Luke and saw that he was asleep. Teddy was ready to be with me again, so I let him come downstairs, took him to my bathroom, and gave him a quick brush out.

"There you go, sweet doggie. Now, let's get you a bit of supper before the guests arrive."

With Teddy taken care of, I lit the candles and looked in the mirror to make sure I had enough lipstick on, just as the doorbell rang. The nurse had arrived, looking quite competent in a blue uniform, gray sweater, and sturdy looking shoes.

"Hello, Mrs. Bradley?" she inquired, in a calm, confident voice. "I'm Dorothy Evans, the night nurse Dr.

Peters ordered."

"How do you do? I'm Jillian. Please come in."

She stepped inside and glanced briefly around, taking in her new surroundings and I ushered her upstairs to Luke's room, making her comfortable in a chair next to a small table outside in the hall. I explained to her that I was giving an engagement party, and she took it in stride. Being an older woman, I felt she must have had lots of experience dealing with different situations. She told me not to worry, took out a book from her large purse, along with a small thermos, which I assumed was filled with coffee, and set them on the table, placing her purse down on the floor alongside of her medical bag.

"I'll peek in on him every thirty minutes to make sure he's all right. Doctor Peters told me what happened. I know what to do, so you run along to your party and leave him to me. I have a grandson just about his age," she said.

Relieved, I took a deep breath and descended the stairs. I had one minute left before the first guest was to arrive.

I tried to get into a festive frame of mind for Walter and Cecilia's sake, but it was difficult. What was I doing getting involved like this? No, Jillian, I said to myself, helping this boy is the right thing to do. I silently prayed to get through this evening calmly, even though I was exhausted and very concerned about the injured girl, and for the boy who was so disoriented.

The caterers informed me that everything was ready, and I took one last look around at the dining room.

I had two round tables set up, festively decorated in red and green tartan for Christmas, since it was only two weeks away. Green moiré tablecloths, skirted to the floor, were topped with centerpieces of fresh pineapples surrounded with pinecones, apples, lemons, and clove studded oranges—all nestled in boughs of greenery and baby's breath, and laced with walnuts and cranberries. The tartan theme was repeated in the brass chandelier, with a few pieces of fruit hanging down, tied with tartan ribbon. I had set up a punch bowl, along with a creamy Brie spread and assorted crackers on the sideboard, decorated in the same manner. Large tartan bows completed the festive arrays. I turned on the gas log, gave a final admiring glance around the house, and looked forward to the party at last.

Cecilia and Walter arrived first, followed by Cecilia's father, Douglas, and Walter's parents, Walter Sr., and his wife Opal. Warm greetings were exchanged, and one of the caterers, whom I had asked beforehand, took their coats and purses and put them in the hall closet.

Cecilia, who normally dressed quite conservatively, looked resplendent in her short red holiday dress. She showed me the engagement ring that Walter had given her—it was simple and elegant, and I told her how beautiful I thought it was. Walter looked very debonair in his new dark suit.

"Merry Christmas, Jillian, and thank you so much for this evening—your home looks gorgeous!"

"Thank you, Walter—it was fun to decorate. You know how I love a pretty house."

"I hope Cecilia and I will have a home like this someday."

The doorbell rang again, and again, until all of the guests had arrived. Walter's former superior officer, Frank Viscuglia and his wife, Margaret, came from Half Moon Bay, as did Jack Anatolia, Walter Sr.'s business partner. Two of my dear Garden Club friends, Ann Fieldman and Nicole King, who both happened to be in town, followed them. Cecilia's managing editor, Ron Iverson and his wife, arrived a few minutes later, followed closely by Prentice Duvall, owner of The Duvall Gallery here in Clover Hills. I had been a loyal customer of his for years, and we had enjoyed each other's company at dinner from time to time. He was very fond of Cecilia and supported her reporting with complimentary letters to the editor.

I wondered what had happened to the best man and maid of honor. I asked Cecilia if they were still coming.

"Josh and Ericka will be just a few minutes late, Jillian," Cecilia said. "He called Walter and said he had to go to a call this afternoon with the fire department. There was a bad accident over in Canyon Grove. He was picking Ericka up."

I chose not to divulge what had happened just yet.

"Why don't we all have a glass of cranberry punch while we wait?" I offered, ushering my guests into the dining room and asking them to excuse me for a moment.

I pulled Walter aside and told him I had a special guest. I asked if he would bring over an outfit for him in the morning, since he and Luke were about the same size. Walter was happy to do so and instantly curious, wanting to know all the details. After explaining some of the situation, Walter wanted talk to Luke at the first opportunity.

"I'll introduce you after Dr. Peters has examined him. I must tell you that I'm uneasy about him, Walter. Is there any way you can help me find his parents?"

Walter looked over at Frank Viscuglia and caught his eye. "I think that can be arranged, Jillian. I'll talk to Frank at the first opportunity."

"Well, for now, let's just enjoy your party. I'm so very happy for both of you. Ah, I hear the doorbell. It's probably Josh and Ericka. Excuse me while I answer it. I'll be right back."

Walter found Cecilia and whispered in her ear. I knew he was telling her about Luke. There were never any secrets between them.

Josh and Ericka joined us, offering profuse apologies for

being late, just as we all sat down for dinner. I wondered if Josh was as tired as I was after dealing with the accident.

The caterers served a lovely dinner of Marinated Tomato Salad, Individual Beef Wellingtons, Whipped Potato Casserole, Baby Sweet Peas with Honey Pecan Butter, and Angel Rolls. Everyone was happily engaged in conversation, exchanging funny vignettes of Walter and Cecilia, and enjoying the delicious meal.

Douglas, Cecilia's father, seated at my right, stood and raised his glass of sparkling cider in a toast to the happy couple. He managed to get through what he wanted to say until he mentioned how sorry he was that Cecilia's mother couldn't be there. We toasted Walter and Cecilia, clicking our glasses together just before Douglas broke down and had to sit down.

Cecilia was sitting on my left, but rose from her chair and went to give her father a hug. He apologized and everyone graciously understood. The table was cleared and coffee and dessert were served—a twelve-layer, Chocolate Cinnamon Torte.

One of the servers came to my table and told me the nurse needed to see me. I excused myself and climbed the stairs to see what was wrong.

"Oh, Mrs. Bradley," she began, "I was checking his pulse right before I was going to give him a sedative, and he woke up and looked at me strangely."

"Yes," I said, "he has amnesia, I think."

"I know, Dr. Peters told me that before I came."

"Then why did you call for me?" I said, just a little irritated at being taken away from my guests.

"It's what he said, ma'am."

"Go on, then," I said, "tell me what he said. I need to get back to my guests."

"He just said, 'He got the stick! He got it!' I gave him

the sedative as quickly as I could, and then I sent for you. It sounded like he remembered something, and I thought you would want to know."

"Thank you, Dorothy. I apologize for being upset with you. You were right to call me."

"He'll sleep now with the medication I gave him. Do you want me to come get you if he says anything else?"

"Yes, I do. We're trying to find his parents. Maybe he was saying someone was going to use a stick on him somehow, I don't know. I need to get back to my guests. I would check on him every fifteen minutes now—just to make sure he's all right."

"All right, ma'am. I brought a thermos of coffee and some sandwiches. I'll be listening out for him until the relief nurse gets here."

"I'll check with you after my guests have left. I think I'll sleep in the room next to him for tonight."

The nurse agreed it would be a good idea.

I came down the stairs and saw Frank Viscuglia waiting for me.

"Care to tell me what's going on, Jillian?" he asked, escorting me back slowly to the dining room. "Walter said you had a mystery guest from this afternoon's car accident over in Canyon Grove. How in the world did you convince the officers to let him go home with you, that's what I'd like to know! Do you realize how much trouble you're letting yourself in for?"

"He's only a boy, Frank. He can't be much older than sixteen. He's lost his memory and has no one else to turn to right now. I just wonder if anyone has reported him missing. Would you find out for me—call someone?"

"I suppose I could. He might be a runaway. There are plenty of them out there. Let me make some calls tomorrow morning, and I'll see what I can find out."

"Thanks, chief. I would also like a report on the injured driver. I'm sure you can find out what hospital she's in. Just like old times, huh?" I said, remembering the case we solved together in Half Moon Bay some years ago.

"Right," he said. "Just like old times, except for the fact that you're out of my jurisdiction. I'll see if I can get Walter to help you. This is his territory now, and I know he would love the opportunity—he thinks you're quite the sleuth, Jillian."

"Thanks, chief. He's coming over in the morning after Luke's physical."

"What? You've already got him working with you!" He laughed and said, "What do you need me for anyway?"

"Well, for starters, I would like for you to check for a missing persons report."

"You got it, Jillian. Oh, here's my lovely wife."

Margaret joined him and gave me a hug goodbye.

"You two are up to something," she said. "I can just tell!"

The guests were handed their coats and purses, and began to leave. Everyone thanked me for a lovely evening and for the special boxes filled with Christmas cookies that I had placed beside their plates. I thanked them in turn for coming and said goodnight. Walter and Cecilia were the last to leave.

"Thank you so much, Jillian, for the lovely engagement party—it was such a nice thing to do for Walter and me. We love you, you know."

"Yes, I know, and I love you both, too, very much. Now, get a good night's sleep, and Walter, I'll see you in the morning."

"Goodnight, Jillian," they said, and walked to their car.

I locked the doors, closed the shutters, and then extinguished the candles. I left the porch lights on, both in front and in back, and decided to leave a light on in the living room as well. I didn't know what to expect during the night, but I certainly wasn't going to trip over anything if something did happen. I turned off the fireplace and went into the kitchen.

The caterers had just finished taking all the dishes to their van and had put the food away, leaving the kitchen spotless. Now that's the way to entertain, I thought. I thanked them for a job well done and handed a check, sealed in an envelope, to the woman in charge.

I turned off the remaining lights and got ready for bed in my bathroom downstairs, listening out for any strange noises. Not hearing any, I decided I was probably overreacting. Teddy lay sprawled out on the bedroom floor, exhausted from his adventure this afternoon. I picked him up, turned off the light, and carried him up the stairs.

The nurse said there were no more incidents with Luke. He had slept quietly since giving him the sedative. I peeked in through the door and confirmed that he was sleeping peacefully.

Nurse Evans took out a sandwich, poured herself a cup of coffee from the thermos, and said goodnight. The relief nurse was due to arrive at seven for the next twelve-hour shift.

I was utterly exhausted—it had been a miracle that I had not collapsed after my ordeal. Thankfully, my adrenalin carried me through throwing an engagement party on top of it.

I went into the guestroom next to Luke's and closed the door. I placed Teddy on a towel at the foot of the bed, set my alarm for 6:00 a.m., and crawled in between the soft percale sheets.

"Goodnight, Lord," I whispered. "Thank you again for sparing the lives of these kids. I pray for the girl, that she'll pull through, and I pray that You will help us find out Luke's identity. Goodnight, Teddy," I murmured, and fell asleep.

4

There was a soft knock on my door. I looked at my clock, and it said 1 a.m. Teddy pricked up his ears and began to yip.

"It's all right, Teddy," I said, putting on my robe and stepping into my slippers.

I opened my door and found the nurse looking distraught.

"What's the matter?" I asked, holding Teddy in my arms.

"You need to come right away — he's talking in his sleep again. I can't make out what he's saying, but I thought you might."

"Of course, when did he get his last sedative?" I asked, wondering how coherent he might be.

"I was just about to give it to him. I'd been checking on him every fifteen minutes, just like you'd asked me to. He's been sound asleep until now."

We reached Luke's room and went in. I put Teddy down at the foot of the bed, and he lay down and went to sleep again as if he wasn't concerned in the slightest. I took that as a good sign that there wasn't anything seriously wrong.

Luke had his eyes closed, but he was moving fitfully about, as if he were having a bad dream.

I listened closely to what he was saying. The nurse listened, too.

It sounded like, "Got to pass the test, try harder, pass the test, make him proud, hard test, must pass...," and then he writhed and moaned as if he was in pain.

"Dorothy, I think you should give him another sedative."

"Yes, ma'am, I'll get it right away."

I sat by Luke's bed and watched him take the medication without even opening his eyes. He was in a deep sleep—perhaps the amnesia had gone deeper.

If he was talking about a test, it must mean he was a student. The need for him to make someone proud suggested that a father was in the picture. Luke wouldn't be going to school tomorrow, I was sure, since he didn't even know who he was. I figured I could call the local high schools the day after tomorrow and check their absentee records. A name might come up that I could check out.

"He seems to have calmed down now," I said. "I think I'll go back to bed. Teddy can stay with him until morning. Come get me if he wakes again."

"I will, ma'am. See you in the morning."

There were no more incidents during the night. My faithful alarm went off at six, and after forcing my eyes to open, I grabbed my glasses, put on my robe and slippers, and went downstairs to make coffee.

I turned off the porch lights and living room light, and

then opened the shutters to greet the mild winter day. I lit the gas log, then went into the kitchen and poured myself a cup of coffee, glancing out the window to see if there was anything unusual. Everything was quiet—just a normal Sunday morning in Clover Hills. I wouldn't be attending church this morning, with Dr. Peters and Walter coming over. I would have to miss it.

I'd better get breakfast on, I thought. I knew Luke was probably starving since he didn't have dinner last night.

I prepared bacon, scrambled eggs, a bowl of fresh berries sprinkled with a little sugar, and biscuits with butter and apricot jam—I would offer him strawberry, too— I didn't know which he would prefer.

I poured him a glass of orange juice and placed everything on a breakfast tray, adding a small pitcher of half-and-half for the berries, in case he should like some. I would bring him a cup of coffee later if he wished.

I went up the stairs carrying the tray, hoping I could serve him before the nurses changing of the guard. It was 6:45 a.m.

The nurse opened the door for me, and I entered Luke's room, carrying the tray, and set it down on the table next to his bed. Teddy stretched and wagged his fluffy little tail, happy to see me. I gave him a hug, and he eyed the food.

I spoke to Teddy loudly enough to wake Luke gently. "This is Luke's breakfast, if he wants to share some with you, it's up to him."

Luke stirred, opened his eyes, and smiled for the second time. He sat up slowly and glanced around the room, until he saw Teddy.

"Good morning, Teddy," he said.

I was happy Luke had remembered his name.

"Good morning, Jillian."

He looked at the breakfast tray.

"Is that for me?"

"It is if you're hungry," I said. "How are you feeling, Luke?"

"My head hurts still, and I feel a little groggy, but I know one thing—I'm starving!"

"I think that sounds good. I need to take Teddy outside for a minute. Why don't you get comfortable and enjoy your breakfast. Would you like me to bring you some coffee, or would you like some hot chocolate, I have that too."

"Hot chocolate sounds great. Thank you, Jillian."

Teddy yipped impatiently, and I knew he needed to go outside.

"We'll be right back," I said. "I'll bring your hot chocolate. There's a new nurse coming in a few minutes. I wanted to make sure you were all right until we can work things out."

"Okay," he said. "I'll see you in a little while."

The changing of the nurse guard took place without much incident, except for my cautioning them to keep Luke's presence confidential. I explained that we were taking every precaution to keep him safe until we found out his identity. I appealed to their professional attitude in the matter, and they agreed wholeheartedly to cooperate.

I made hot chocolate for Luke and took it to him. He had eaten every morsel of the breakfast I had made for him, and it made me feel good.

"That was the best breakfast, Jillian. You cook good like…like…."

"Like who, Luke?"

"I can't remember. It just won't come."

"But you do remember that someone cooks for you—I think that's a start.

"Last night, you mentioned that you had to pass a test. Do you know what test you have to pass, Luke?"

"A test?" he asked. "I can't think of any test, but that means I must be in school, right?"

"Yes, that's what that means. You also mentioned that you have to make *him* proud. Can you think who it is you want to make proud?"

Luke closed his eyes, trying to think, but his face fell as he opened them again, and looked at me.

"I can't see anyone in my mind. It's like there's nothing there except darkness."

The doorbell rang. It must have been Dr. Peters.

"Excuse me, Luke. I need to get the door. I'm having Dr. Peters take a look at you to see what we need to do to get your memory back. I'll take the tray downstairs and be back in a minute. You lie down and relax, okay?"

"Okay. And thanks for the breakfast," he said, politely.

Someone has taught this boy excellent manners, I thought.

Dr. Peters was a quiet man who had lost his wife to cancer. He was slightly built, but possessed a huge intellect, a man who enjoyed his work as a physician, one who constantly studied new discoveries in the medical field. I felt extremely fortunate to have him for my personal physician, as well as a friend. He looked at Luke with keen inquisitiveness, decidedly interested in his case.

"Let's take a look at you and see what's going on," he said. After the examination, Dr. Peters instructed Luke to rest, and then spoke to the nurse, giving her instructions on Luke's care. I invited him downstairs to discuss Luke's case over a cup of coffee.

"How about some biscuits and jam?" I offered.

"I don't think I can resist, Jillian," he laughed, taking two, and slathering them with butter and apricot jam.

"Dr. Peters, Luke...."

"So he knows his name, does he?" Dr. Peters said,

surprised.

"Oh, no, he just chose that name temporarily so I'd have something to call him. He's only said a few things about what he remembers, and only one was when he was awake. What do you think, Doctor?" I asked.

Dr. Peters took a bite of his biscuit, and set it down.

"The young man definitely has amnesia. I can't tell you whether it will be for a short time or a very long time. There is no way to really tell. Judging by his bone size, I can tell you, however, that he's about seventeen years old. He's in good health, other than the concussion he's suffered, and his teeth are perfect—he's never had a filling. I'll need to do an x-ray to learn anything else. Can you bring him to my office sometime this morning?"

"If you think he's stable enough. Would you like more coffee, Dr. Peters?"

"I would love some. Thank you, its excellent coffee, Jillian."

I poured us both more coffee, and asked what I should do to take care of Luke. He told me to make sure he got lots of rest and good food to keep his strength up, and make sure he took his medication at night to make him sleep.

"I really need to be going, Jillian. Take good care of our patient, and I'll tell the office to expect you this morning." He wrote a lab request, handed it to me, and then stood to leave.

"Thank you again for the delicious biscuits and coffee. Luke's in very good hands, if you ask me."

"I appreciate your coming over, doctor. I'll talk to you after we get the lab work done. Goodbye now."

"I'll see you later, Jillian."

I called Walter the minute Dr. Peters left.

"I'll be there in fifteen minutes, Jillian," he said. "I have some information for you, but you'll have to wait until I get there. Everything go okay last night?" he asked.

"You'll have to wait until you get here," I joked back, "see you in a few minutes."

I emptied the dishwasher, put out some turkey and cheese for Teddy, made sure he had fresh water, and finished cleaning up the kitchen.

I ran to my bedroom, made my bed, placing the throw pillows against the headboard in the right order, and got dressed.

Fortunately, Walter had taken twenty minutes instead of fifteen so I was all ready by the time he rang the doorbell.

"Come in, come in. It's good to see you, Walter."

He handed me a pile of neatly folded clothes.

"These are for Luke?" I asked.

He nodded, and asked, "So, what happened last night?"

I told him everything Luke had said in his sleep on both occasions, and the comment he made about the cooking.

"I'm taking him for x-rays this morning. Would you like to come along?" I invited.

"I would, indeed. Now, would you like to hear about what I've found out?"

"I would, indeed," I said. "Is there a missing persons report?"

"There was just one—for a girl named Madison Sanders. Her father called when she didn't come home last night. I called him after I got home from the party. He said they never had any problems before. I had to tell them about the accident she was in, and they fell apart. They've been at the hospital with her ever since."

"How is she?" I asked.

"Not good. I went over there earlier this morning and tried to talk to her, but she was still unconscious."

"That poor girl!"

"She hasn't said a word to anyone, and she looks awful.

The doctor said she has several broken ribs and a punctured lung, which he said was a cause for concern. Her face was cut up badly from all the broken glass, and she was burned on both of her legs from the explosion."

"Her parents have to be beside themselves. We need to talk to them as soon as possible. Do you know how to reach them?"

"Yeah, they own a boarding stable over in Canyon Grove. I got all the information."

"Good work, Walter. What about the car she was driving?"

"Now that's a problem. I talked to forensics, and they said it would take a few days to even *find* the VIN since the car was blown apart. The pieces have to all be retrieved and examined before they can give us any information. Don't worry, though, I'm going to call them every day until they come up with something."

"That's the right spirit. I also need to tell you that I saw two men chasing their car right before it crashed."

"Why didn't you say something, Jillian! That's got to be important!"

"Well, it's not like I didn't have anything else to think about, with your engagement party and a houseguest to take care of right after rendering aid in a car accident!"

"Point taken—I apologize for not thinking," Walter said sincerely.

"Oh, it's all right. I know you're just as anxious as I am to find out what this is all about. I forgive you."

"Well, you were saying about these two men that were following them…."

"The car Luke was in was speeding and ran a stop sign before turning onto Benito Canyon Road. This other car, a black sedan, and a luxury car I think, was following them, and ran the stop sign as well. When the kids' car turned over and went over into the ravine, the men stopped and got out of their car, just as I was pulling up. When they saw me, they got back into their car and sped off. Talk about acting guilty!"

"You didn't get their plate number, by any chance?"

"Teddy wanted me to...."

"Teddy wanted you to? Sorry, I forgot about his special instincts. Go on."

"I was going to write it down, but they drove off in such a hurry I didn't have a chance. I knew I should help the crash victims first, so Teddy and I got to them as fast as we could.

"The paramedics took the girl to the hospital, and I offered to bring Luke home with me until we could figure out who he was. That's the story. Well, it was up until last night."

"And Luke talked in his sleep," Walter reiterated.

He poured himself a cup of coffee, I got a refill, and we sat down at the kitchen table together. He took out a small device and began making notes.

"I need to record what the nurse said, so give it to me again, if you would be so kind."

"The nurse told me that during the night, Luke said 'He got the stick, he got it!' and he 'needed to pass the test,' he 'needed to try harder,' and that he 'wanted to make some man proud.'"

"He also said something about cookies?"

"Not cookies, *cooking*. When he told me I was a good cook, it reminded him of someone, but he couldn't remember who it was.

"I asked him about what he said during the night, and it made no sense to him. We may find out more after the x-rays are taken."

"When do we take him in?"

"Right now, actually. I really need to get him ready — thanks for the clothes. I'll see that you get them back."

"Hey, I was glad to help. I think I should meet him — it might help if I gained his confidence. I'm concerned that these men were following two kids like this. It might be drug related."

"That's why I want the lab work done as soon as possible. The more we know about Luke, the more we'll know how to help him find his way home."

"Oh, there was one more thing, Jillian, before we talk to Luke."

"What is it?"

"Well, I talked to the officer at the crash site, and he told me he submitted a request for fingerprints and footprints for Luke on his computer, since he claimed he didn't know who he was. We have that capability now, if you didn't know."

"I assumed, but didn't know for sure," I said, knowing how sophisticated police equipment is now days.

"Evidently, this boy didn't have a driver's license or a criminal record. In fact, the officer didn't find any record at all, not even a birth record."

"Well, not having a criminal record is in his favor, anyway. Walter, do you realize, that if we don't help him find out who he is, his life could be ruined forever? I've read about amnesia victims, and I know what I'm talking about."

"I've thought about it, sure, and I agree with you. I think it's time I met Luke."

❧5❧

The nurse was helping Luke get dressed when Walter and I got to his room.

"Luke, I have someone I'd like you to meet. He's a good friend of mine, and he wants to help you."

Walter stepped forward and extended his hand.

"Hello, Luke, I'm Walter Montoya."

"Walter is a police detective here in Clover Hills. If anyone can help find out who you are, it's Walter."

Luke looked at Walter and then at me.

"That sounds good. It's a pleasure to meet you, sir."

"Excuse me," Walter said, answering his phone, "I'll be right there. Follow procedure."

"What is it? What's happened?" I asked, sensing it wasn't good.

"There's been a homicide over in Canyon Grove. I have to go right now. Take the nurse with you to get the lab work, and, Jillian, make sure there's someone else with you and Luke at all times. This homicide may not be a coincidence with Luke here—I don't want to take any chances. I'll call you when I get more information. I have to leave now. Luke, it was nice to meet you. I'll be talking with you soon."

"Goodbye, Walter, and be careful. Call me as soon as you can, okay?"

"I will, and you two be careful as well."

"Come on Luke—let's go see what we can find out about you at the lab."

"He's all ready ma'am," the nurse said.

Luke stared out the car window during the short trip to the lab. It was as if he was seeing Clover Hills for the first time.

"Does any of this look familiar?" I asked.

He simply shook his head, no. "Jillian, why do you take Teddy with you? Why don't you just leave him at home?"

"Teddy was kidnapped once—it was a long time ago, but I still can't let him out of my sight. If I can't take him with me, I make sure he's with someone I trust, which is usually Cecilia. She's my personal assistant whenever I need her."

"That's how I feel sometimes," he said.

"Like a personal assistant?" I queried.

"No, like what you said about Teddy. I think there's someone like that who watches me, like you watch Teddy. I wish I knew who it was. Do you think they're looking for me?"

I knew there had not been a missing persons report as far as I knew. I'm sure Walter would have told me if there were.

Why wouldn't someone be looking for this wonderful boy? He was nice looking, polite, intelligent, and composed as far as I could see. It didn't make any sense at all.

"They must be looking for you. I would be if you were my son."

"Do you have any kids, Jillian?" he asked.

I smiled in the rearview mirror at the nurse, who was listening intently, I could tell.

"No, my husband was killed in Vietnam, many years ago. It happened before we had any children. I do have two nieces and two nephews, though."

"I think they're lucky to have an aunt like you," Luke said.

The nurse smiled and nodded in agreement.

The lab work was performed and x-rays were taken. Dr. Peters had promised to discuss them immediately, instead of making us wait. He was sensitive to the fact that we needed to find out who this boy was as soon as we could. We sat in his waiting room until he could see us.

My phone rang, startling all three of us.

"Jillian, its Walter, just listen to what I have to tell you. A man was found murdered this morning over here, right here in the middle of Main Street. Actually, we found him in the clutches of an old hay grappler hanging from the rafters of the Mercantile Barn, right in plain view! I don't think this is a coincidence. No one *ever* gets murdered in Canyon Grove!"

"How do you know, Walter? Never mind the question. Did you get an identification?"

Luke sensed something was wrong.

"What happened?" he asked.

I told Walter to hang on.

"A man has been found dead over in Canyon Grove. I'm trying to find out who it is."

The nurse said, "Canyon Grove? That's where my brother lives. Please find out who it is, ma'am."

"I'm sorry, Walter, who was it?"

"A man named Quentin Graves."

She looked at me with concern.

"Ma'am," she said, "Who was it?"

"A man named Quentin Graves," I answered, watching her reaction. I glanced at Luke's as well.

"Was that your brother?" I asked reluctantly.

"No, thank God!" she said, breathing a sigh of relief. "But I know I've heard that name before—I just can't think where."

"Let me know if it comes to you, I would appreciate it," I said, reaching into my purse and taking a business card from my silver card case, "here's how to reach me."

"Yes, ma'am, I certainly will."

Nurse Turner had a burdened look on her face. I wondered if she knew more about Quentin Graves than she was telling us.

"I'm sorry, Walter. Nurse Turner's brother lives in Canyon Grove, and she needed to know who the victim was."

"I can certainly understand. I did some checking and found he had a record, but it was a long time ago, so it may take some time to figure out who killed him," Walter said.

"I think what may be more important now is *why* he was killed. How did he die, Walter?" I asked.

Both Luke and the nurse were watching my face as Walter described the brutal beating and throat slashing that the victim had suffered.

I winced and closed my eyes in pity for the man.

"It sounds like he was punished for something he did," I thought aloud.

"Walter, the doctor just came in. I'll call you as soon as we've talked to him. I'll talk to you later."

Dr. Peters had a look of concern on his face as he sat down to talk to us.

"Nurse Turner," he began, "I think Luke is going to need home care for at least a couple of weeks to make sure he gets the rest and medications he needs."

"I'll be happy to care for him, doctor," she replied.

"Jillian," Dr. Peters continued, "Luke is going to need plenty of love and care if he's going to get over his amnesia. He's suffered what we call traumatic amnesia from his head injury. There's no cure—just treatment and luck. Are you willing to take on this responsibility?"

"Yes, I am. I think Nurse Turner and I can take care of him. She'll need the relief nurse at night, so perhaps you should order one when you talk to your nurse. How long does it take to get over something like this?" I asked.

Dr. Peters looked at Luke and smiled a half-smile of encouragement. I appreciated the sensitive manner in which he included Luke in the discussion.

"A lot depends on the severity of the concussion. Sometimes a patient will recall older memories first and never recall the moments before the trauma. Some patients gradually recall everything. Every case is different.

It's actually very unusual for a patient, such as Luke, not to remember who he is, even though he doesn't remember anything else. He may remember his identity at any time, so be prepared in case it happens.

I'll want him to get a lot of rest. If there is a problem, I'll give you a refill prescription for the sedatives."

Teddy lay down on the floor and decided he needed his morning nap.

I watched as Dr. Peters opened a folder he had prepared, containing a file of Luke's lab results.

"Now, according to the blood work, we know he is type AB positive, which is very rare. It means one parent has blood type A positive, and the other has type B positive. I think Luke is lucky. All we need to do to confirm who his parents are is to find a couple with these blood types."

"Who happen to be missing a child of Luke's description," I added. "I think this will be helpful."

"There's more," Dr. Peters resumed.

Luke was listening thoughtfully. I could tell he was processing the information in a rational manner.

"There is no indication of him ever having a broken bone—no fractures; in fact, I would have to say he is in perfect health, except for his concussion and some bruising on his shoulder. He's even in better health than most young people are. This indicates to me that he has been very well taken care of."

"You mean, he's been fed well, and had all his immunizations, things of that nature?" I asked.

"I would assume he's had good nutrition. We can only tell if he's immune to certain diseases, like chickenpox, for example, and certain people are naturally immune, so it wouldn't be conclusive to say if he had received a vaccination for it, unless there was a record."

"Which we don't have, of course," I interjected.

"There is only one unusual thing we found in the x-ray."

Luke became alert at the mention of something unusual. I knew it must have been hope of finding a clue to his identity.

"What did you find?" Luke asked.

Dr. Peters clipped an x-ray to a light board on the wall next to his computer. It was taken showing his upper right torso. Dr. Peters pointed out a tiny capsule, about the size of a grain of rice just beneath Luke's back shoulder.

"This is a microchip of some kind." I can remove it without too much trouble if you would like. It will only take a few minutes."

Luke looked at me for reassurance and then at Dr.

Peters.

"Will it hurt?" he asked.

"I don't think so. I'll be giving you a local anesthetic. Would you like me to remove it, Luke? I'll just need Jillian's permission, since she's your temporary guardian."

"Yeah," Luke said. "I don't want that thing in me. Is it all right with you, Jillian?"

"I agree. It may give us a clue to who you are, so I'm all in favor. Anytime, Dr. Peters."

"I'll call the nurse to have everything prepared, and I'll have her call in Luke's refill. I'll also order the night nurse. You'll have to excuse me for a moment."

Dr. Peters left the room, and I patted Luke on his good shoulder.

"Everything is going to work out, Luke. It's going to be all right."

I took out my phone. "I need to call Walter—I'm sure he'll find this of great interest."

I could tell from Luke's face that he didn't like finding out he'd been micro-chipped, and Teddy sensed something was wrong. He got up and went to Luke, pawing his leg, indicating he wanted to sit in his lap. Luke picked him up and gave him a hug.

"Jillian," he said, "don't they put microchips in pets to be able to find them? I know I've read about it, or maybe I heard someone talking about it, I'm not sure which, but I know what they are."

"Yes, in fact Teddy has one. I had it put in after he was kidnapped to make sure I could find him...."

Walter answered my call.

"Hello, Walter. I have a bit of news about Luke. It appears he has been micro-chipped. Have you ever heard of such a thing in humans?"

"We need to talk, Jillian. That doesn't sound good at all.

41

I really don't think Luke needs to hear what I have to say about it, so why don't I meet you back at your house. Is the nurse still there?"

"Yes, Dr. Peters said she should stay on until Luke is recovered. He's going to remove the microchip right now. I'll bring it with me so you can have it checked out."

"That sounds good. Listen, I'm calling Cecilia to come stay with you, too. You're not used to the extra work it will mean. Ron will understand. In fact, he'll want the story for his paper after we find out Luke's identity, so it shouldn't be a problem. I'm also going to have an officer watch your house. I don't have a good feeling about this whole thing. Stay at the lab until I can get there, and I'll escort you home. I'm calling Cecilia now. I'll see you in twenty-minutes."

"Thanks, Walter. I feel a whole lot safer. We'll watch for your car. Goodbye." Luke was watching my face as I ended my call, and I could tell he was troubled by the fear in his eyes.

"Walter is coming to see us home safely," I told him, reassuringly.

"There's something bad about me, isn't there, Jillian?" Luke said, crestfallen.

"It may not be bad about you, Luke, but it may mean that you might be a person who is around bad people. There is a big difference, and we're going to believe the best about you."

"Until you find out the truth," he sulked.

"Hey, I'm not giving up on you. I think you're much too nice to be a bad person," I said. What I was thinking, though, was that I hoped he was not involved in something sinister.

Dr. Peters finished removing the microchip and applied a bandage over the incision. I glanced out the window and saw Walter's unmarked patrol car pull into a parking space in front of the office.

"Here's Walter now, thank you for seeing us so soon, Dr. Peters."

"You're welcome. Let me know if I can help in any way. You should bring him back in about a week and let me see how his shoulder is doing—just make an appointment on your way out."

"It will be Christmas in two weeks. I hope we know who he is by then. That's the only thing I want, really," I mused.

Walter helped us into my car and followed us home. Luke said nothing—he just held Teddy in his arms and rested his head on Teddy's. At least Luke has one friend that he feels doesn't judge him, I thought.

Cecilia was waiting for us in the living room when we walked in the front door. I had given her a key to my house years ago, so she could come and go without having to disturb me in case I was working on my column and needed no interruptions. I trusted her completely. I introduced her to Luke and Nurse Turner.

"I'm glad to know you, Luke. How do you do Nurse Turner?" said Cecilia.

"Oh, please call me Amanda."

"I will."

She looked at Luke, not sure how to make him out because he looked so sullen.

"How do you do?" Luke said, his mind still on the microchip, I could tell.

Cecilia said, "I brought my laptop and some video games that I thought you might like to play when you feel like it."

Luke's face lit up, and I knew he and Cecilia would get along just fine.

"Cecilia, why don't you take Luke upstairs with

Amanda and Teddy, and make sure they're comfortable. Maybe he would like to play on the computer or watch TV. Is that all right, Jillian?" asked Walter.

I knew he wanted to talk to me alone.

"It's fine with me," I said. "Cecilia, you know where everything is, I'll make us some lunch in a little while and call you when it's ready."

I noticed Luke's face brighten a little when I mentioned food. At least he still had his appetite. I led Walter to the living room and offered him some coffee.

"In a little while, thanks, Jillian," he said.

I knew it was serious if Walter declined my coffee. I handed Walter the microchip Dr. Peters had removed from Luke's shoulder and had placed in a small plastic container.

"Let's have it, Walter. What's this microchip all about?" I asked, as I got myself a cup of coffee.

He sighed and crossed his right leg over his left, looking closely at the rice-sized chip.

"Microchips are still in the early stages of being tested on humans. They're used in animals to keep track of them and they work well, as long as someone will take the animal to a vet that can scan the chip for a read-out."

"I see," I said. "So far, so good, go on."

"As far as actually tracking an animal to find its whereabouts if it gets lost — that hasn't fully been developed yet."

I took a sip of coffee and placed the mug on a coaster, looking at Walter and giving him my undivided attention,

"Go on, Walter."

"Microchips in human beings are still a very controversial subject. On one hand, some people think it would be convenient for everyone to have one because it would eliminate the need for plastic cards to carry around to make purchases with, and it might eliminate identity theft…things like that. On the other hand, it would be an invasion of privacy if people could be tracked for any reason whatsoever, and whether they liked it or not."

"I would tend to agree. Besides, what if a person chose not to be micro-chipped for that very reason, and lost their ability to buy and sell?"

"I know what you're getting at—the end times and mark of the beast. That's been one of the big objections in going forward with their development. However, that's not to say some entities haven't been actively developing their capabilities. The reason I was so surprised to hear about Luke's having one, is that just two weeks ago, we found a murder victim over in Tracy who had something cut out of her back shoulder, right where you told me Luke's was."

I sat up straighter in my chair.

"How do you know it wasn't a stab wound?" I asked.

"Her throat had been slit. There were no other wounds. The killer dumped her body in one of the canals. We've found several like that, but she was the first one to have an incision like that."

"Who was she?"

"We weren't able to get an ID on her—she didn't have any record, but we think she was an illegal. The description said she was a Jane Doe with brown hair and brown eyes. Estimated age was twenty. No tattoos or other identifying marks—she was found nude so the killer made sure there weren't any articles of clothing or personal items to trace."

"That's horrible," I said, feeling a little sickened at how she must have suffered. "She was so young! I wonder if she was a prostitute."

"It's hard to tell. There were no reports that alluded to it. I don't think anyone would report it anyway—no one wants to be mixed up with the police if they were involved like that."

"You're probably right, especially if no one reported her missing."

Walter told me of other cases like hers, some young women, and some middle-aged men—all unidentified and all assumed to be illegals. I wondered why someone would murder illegals. Did they have incriminating information on their importers? Did they not pay for their entry into this country? Were they involved in drugs somehow? I suppose there was no way to ask them if they were dead. And why dump their bodies in the Tracy canals, unless it was close and convenient.

"I'm telling you, Jillian, that boy is tied up in this somehow. I think he's actually lucky to have had that accident like he did, otherwise, he may have never had another chance."

"You're saying he might have been running away from something he was involved in, aren't you?"

"It could be. But I do know, that micro-chipping someone in this day and age means control, and that, my dear friend, is definitely illegal."

"But can someone be injected of their own free will, I wonder."

"There have been a few cases like that. However, the ones who have injected *themselves* for instance, have injected their hands, not their backs. No, someone injected Luke— we have to find out *why.*"

❧6❧

I prepared a luncheon for the four of us, since Walter was called away on the Quentin Graves case. I knew Luke would be hungry, as most teenage boys are. Dr. Peters had said Luke looked like he had eaten well. I assumed there was a mother figure somewhere that was making sure he did. I made some turkey and cheese sandwiches, with a side of potato chips, and glasses of milk. I thought it would be best if I took Luke's on a tray so he could rest afterwards, as Dr. Peters had suggested. I put a small plate of extra turkey and a few bites of cheese on the tray, so Luke could share with Teddy without having to give up part of his lunch.

"Here's your lunch," I said, as I entered Luke's room. There was a moment where he almost looked happy. I'm sure it was because he had Cecilia for company, and I was bringing lunch.

"We'll take ours downstairs so you can get some rest," I said, placing the tray on his lap. "I brought a little extra for

Teddy if he starts begging. You know I spoil him!"

"He's still a great dog," Luke said, giving Teddy a few loving pats.

Teddy pulled his ears back, basking in the affection.

"Thanks for the lunch, Jillian. I was really hungry. I'm sorry for being so down."

"Hey, you've been through quite an ordeal, young man. Now don't worry about anything, just eat your lunch and rest some more. I'll come get your tray in a few minutes and check on you. Nurse Turner is right outside your door."

Cecilia and I made our way downstairs and into the kitchen, where I had lunch set up on the table.

"I understand we have a man looking out for us outside, did Walter tell you?" I asked.

"Yes, he told me. What are you going to do? I know you're not going to just sit here and do nothing."

"Walter told me to always have another person with me when I was with Luke. Well, if I don't have Luke with me, then I don't need another person, do I?"

"What are you saying?"

"If I leave Luke here with you and Nurse Turner, and there's a man outside watching the house, that means Luke has more than two people watching him. I think that's what Walter had in mind. I need to go to Canyon Grove and see if I can find out anything. I promised Verity LaBelle I would come over and discuss my rose workshop for next month. I think this would be a perfect time to do it. You stay with Luke, and I'll let Walter know where I'm going. That way, he can give our tail a head's up. Oh my, did I just make a pun?" I laughed.

"If you think it's best to leave me here, I'm game. I think that under the circumstances, it's better to have someone here who knows your house, in case the nurse needs something. I guess Luke and I can always play cards if he gets bored. Now, you stay in touch after you leave LaBelle's so I'll know you're all right, okay?"

"Okay, I'll call you. I want to see how Luke is doing anyway. I'd better give Verity a call to let her know I'm on my way. Thanks for helping, Cecilia. I really don't know what I'd do without you."

"You had better never try, Jillian! Now you had better give Verity a call and get going. I'll get Luke's tray and clean up the kitchen. Don't worry about that."

"You're an angel, Cecilia. Thanks. I'll call you soon. Be sure and let Teddy out in a few minutes, okay?"

"Okay, I'll talk to you soon."

Verity said to come anytime, and looked forward to chatting about the workshop. I pulled into the gorgeous nursery that the LaBelle sisters had owned and operated for forty years.

It stood close to downtown Canyon Grove on a sizable piece of property. Their nursery attracted gardeners from all over the Bay Area, and it was no wonder. Not only did LaBelle's carry the finest quality plants and trees, there was a gift shop, café, and a small conference center where I would be holding my workshop.

"Jillian, how nice of you to come," Verity greeted me warmly, as I walked into the main entrance. Her keen gray eyes peered from a wrinkled face, weather worn from working outside all these years. She was smartly dressed in a long-sleeved shirt and slacks, and had on her green LaBelle's Nursery apron, proudly bearing her nametag.

"Where's Teddy?"

"Teddy's at home with Cecilia today. I'll tell him you asked."

We strolled through rows of pansies, snapdragons, and colorful petunias.

"I'm never prepared for the amazing beauty I see when

I come to your nursery, Verity. It's food for my soul!" I said, giving her a hug.

"God has blessed us to be able to work doing what we love most. I love the customer side the business, and Hope immerses herself in the business end of it. It works well for both of us. Now, Jillian, you must come take a look at the new bare root roses that just came in."

I followed her to the rose section at the back.

"I suppose you've heard about our murder this morning."

"As a matter of fact, I have. They found him clutched in a hay grappler of some sort?" I asked.

"I saw it with my own eyes. One of my workers told me about it, and I rushed right over to see it. There he was, lying on his back in that old hay grappler with his arms and legs sticking out. Someone had put him in there and pulled it up by the ropes so everyone would see it. It was gruesome! His face was beaten in so badly that it was barely recognizable. We could see blood on the sidewalk where some of it dripped out beneath his body."

"It makes me shiver just hearing that," I said.

Verity continued her colorful narrative.

"I talked to a woman who was there at the scene — she's one of my customers, and she said she had seen him at the Jazz Cafe a few times when she and her husband had gone there for dinner on the weekends. It's a pretty small restaurant you know."

"I've never been there before."

"Well, it's nice when they have the music on the weekends. You should go sometime."

"I think I will. I wonder if you would give me the name of the woman you talked with. I think the police might want to talk to her."

"Why of course, her name is Mary Stewart. She lives in

Canyon grove, has for years. I could get you her address if you'll wait just a moment."

"Thanks, Verity. Did you know the victim?"

"Not personally, of course, but I heard through the grapevine that he lived in Clover Hills—a man named Quentin Graves. It was rumored that he was involved in the mob somehow, but no one supplied any other details. At least he wasn't from around here."

"But he was murdered here, and obviously, someone made it a point that people in Canyon Grove would be the ones to see his body." I said.

"I suppose you're right. Do you think it was a warning of some kind?"

"It could be. Has anything ever happened here that might point to that?" I asked.

"Not that I know of, however, Hope would know if anyone would. She runs our museum, you know."

"No, I didn't know. Well, let's get on with your questions about my workshop. I brought the outline of what I'll be speaking on."

"I do apologize, Jillian, but I see some customers milling about looking for help. I'll look at this and get back to you. Thank you for coming over. By the way, the museum is right on Main Street, next to the little white church. You can't miss it. Hope is usually there from noon 'til three. I'll e-mail you my questions, all right?"

"That will be perfect. I'll be in touch."

Before I left the nursery, I called Walter and told him I had a lead on Quentin Graves from Verity.

"Let's have it!" he said anxiously.

"It's just a name—a Mary Stewart. Verity talked to her at the crime scene, and evidently, the woman knew Quentin by sight from seeing him at the Jazz Cafe a few times. It might be worth talking to her. I have the address if you're interested."

"By all means, I'll check it out right away."

I pulled out of LaBelle's and made a right turn onto Main Street, looking closely at the businesses along the way.

Canyon Grove reminded me of a movie set of an old western town. I could picture the town in its heyday — women, dressed in long dresses and bonnets, riding in wagons, shopping at the mercantile for home goods, while the men would go into the saloon for a drink. The town was quiet now, almost a ghost town, but not quite. No, a man was murdered in this town by someone very real.

I passed over the railroad tracks and recalled that the Benito Canyon Railway still had a working station here. People took train rides into the canyon for scenic trips on the weekends. I noted the station a block to my right as I crossed the tracks.

The first building I saw on the right was a large, wooden building painted red with white trim, called Canyon Grove Whistle Stop Antiques. On my left stood a small Mission style building, touting itself as the Canyon Grove Coffee House and Café. The word Café was printed on a red and white striped awning over the front door. I noticed the windows were covered in paper, and a man, holding a drawing of some kind, was perusing the property. I judged he was the new proprietor by the looks of his Mercedes parked in front. A watchtower was perched behind the coffee shop. I wondered if people used it to watch for the train, or to watch each other, perhaps.

I slowed down at the next building I came to. It was the large gray mercantile barn, and I stared in horror at the large hay grappler. Four large hooks protruded from the base of an iron triangle, waiting open-mouthed for the next bale of hay to be loaded and hoisted into the barn. It had been raised by a pulley, and suspended from a wooden gallows over the top of the entrance of the mercantile, looking as if no murder had taken place at all.

A large two-storied wooden structure, built right next to the mercantile barn, contained the remainder of businesses that were located along the left-hand side of Main Street.

At the beginning of the structure, a door stood open to a convenience store, with large posters of Coca-Cola and Haagen-Dazs ice cream bars plastered on the windows, bidding tourists and local workers to come in for a snack and a cold drink.

An old wooden hitching post, left over from the days of horse riders, was still in place. It never dawned on me that riders still used it.

An old wooden park bench sat next to the hitching post, inviting those in no hurry to sit and chat with a friend or a fellow tourist.

I knew the train did weekend tours through the canyon, and although I had never ridden a steam engine, it sounded like fun. I wondered whom I could ask to come with me, and thought of Prentice Duvall. Well, *maybe* he would enjoy it, although, he *was* very sophisticated and might enjoy the Napa wine train, instead.

I noticed a small real estate office next to the convenience store as I continued to drive slowly through the tiny town, and saw that the Hill View Hotel occupied the major space. It looked like it was straight out of an old western movie, complete with an iron sign that read SALOON hanging over the entrance door.

The final business establishment in the building was the Canyon Grove Conference Center and Jazz Café. A large wrap-around covered patio, furnished with black patio furniture and market umbrellas, was where the locals and weekend tourists came together for an evening of good food and jazz — alfresco. I was enticed to come see for myself, but wondered how it would be to come alone, as I so often did, being a widow.

Glancing across the street, I saw a community park where the Sheriff's Office and Post Office stood side by side. I could see the train station a few yards down, on an adjacent side street.

I continued driving slowly past the park and saw the church steeple rise up on the right hand side of the street, right next to The Canyon Grove Historical Museum.

I pulled into the parking lot and took a quick look around. The only person I saw was a county official of some kind, wearing a tan Stetson and uniform, getting into a utility truck and driving slowly out of town.

This was as close to a ghost town as I had ever seen, and I'd seen a few. I looked forward to talking to Hope LaBelle and learning what brought people to live in this small community in the first place.

The musty smell of old documents and artifacts wafted through the air as I stepped into the dimly lit museum. I saw Hope, bustling in a back office, looking at a folder of some kind. She didn't even notice me come in. I walked through the main room, filled with sepia photographs of Canyon Grove and its townsfolk, and I glanced at a few articles of clothing and accessories, worn in days long ago by prominent citizens, that were displayed in several glass cases, until Hope looked up and finally noticed my presence.

When she saw me, she removed her glasses from her face, allowing them to dangle from a chain she wore around her neck.

I couldn't help comparing the differences between the two sisters. Whereas Verity was outgoing and people oriented, Hope was introverted and preferred working alone. Verity was very fashionable in her choice of dress, but Hope was content to wear plain and sensible clothing. Because Hope had lived indoors for the most part, her skin was still quite smooth, with only a few crows' feet around her eyes and mouth. She wore no makeup.

"Do come in, Jillian," she said in her quiet voice, as if I had just entered a library.

"I'm so happy to be able to show you around. I suppose you heard about the poor fellow that was murdered last night—I still can't believe it—right here in Canyon Grove. There hasn't been a murder here since…." Hope lost her train of thought and looked troubled.

"I'm sorry, Jillian," she continued, "I'm still shaken by the whole incident."

"You said there hasn't been a murder here since what?" I probed.

"I want to show you something," she said, moving to a family portrait of early residents.

"This is the Edwards family."

She began pointing to each member and describing who they were.

"Uriah Edwards originally owned the land where Canyon Grove stands today. Originally, it was part of a large ranch, a land grant, owned by a wealthy Spanish landowner. After Uriah purchased it, he named it Canyon Grove because of the canyon it sits at the bottom of, and for the groves of olives he cultivated. Uriah was an ambitious rancher—and a very profitable one."

Hope then pointed to the woman standing next to him in the picture.

"He married Rebecca, the daughter of a wealthy neighboring rancher in 1903, and together they had four sons, one of which died in infancy. Their marriage was a happy one, or so we believe when reading the logs Uriah kept, which described his business dealings and day to day events."

"It sounds like he was a very capable business man," I said in admiration.

"In those days," she continued, "as is still the mode here in California's agribusiness today, migrant workers from Mexico were brought in by rail to work these large ranches. Most of the time, it was equitable for both the rancher and the worker, although in those early days there were no unions to protect workers' rights for treatment or pay. I mentioned *murder* earlier, because I believe, according to some other records I've found, Uriah was indirectly responsible for the deaths of several workers and may have even murdered some of them.

"That *is* interesting. Do the records say how they died?"

"I believe some of them were mistreated and died as slaves, while others died of heatstroke, being forced to work in inhuman conditions. I found notations by Uriah that named the worker followed by the letters *DSCD-DSPDC* and then the date."

"*DSCD-DSPDC?*" It could be 'deceased' and 'disposed' but I don't know what the 'C' would stand for."

"I couldn't come up with anything either, but I agree on the deceased and disposed meanings. I think you'll come to the conditions of death when you read the diary of what went on in the household and in the fields, but according to two different accounts, one from the county sheriff at that time and another from a prominent citizen's diary we have, two workers were severely beaten and had their throats slit."

"Just like our recent victim. You might be right. Maybe they are linked somehow."

"It could be a coincidence. But then again, I can't shake

this feeling I have."

"Maybe the victims are calling to you from the grave."

"Maybe they are. But if anyone can see the connection, Jillian, it's you. They may be buried somewhere on the property, or he may have disposed of them some other way. The problem is that it happened so long ago, and at the time, no one considered the migrant workers as human beings with rights, therefore, nothing was done about it, and Uriah continued building his ranching empire with no one to answer to."

"You said you thought this tied in with last night's murder, but how?"

"I was only laying the background by telling you Uriah's story."

She led me to a picture a few rows down from the family portrait. In the picture, a beautiful brick house sat nestled among large oak trees.

"This is the house that Uriah built for his bride, Rebecca. You can see that was a labor of love by all the brick he had brought in, and all the custom framing of the windows."

"I assume they heated the house with fireplaces, since I can see five chimneys here," I said, looking at the photograph and admiring the stately three-storied structure.

"Uriah recorded all the specifications in his log, so we know it was a magnificent house at one time, and one of the few that wasn't destroyed by fire."

"Does anyone live there now?" I asked.

"No one knows for sure. After Uriah and Rebecca died, their son Dorian was said to have occupied the house with his bride, Elsa. The log tells us that Dorian's two brothers chose to take their inheritance and go out into the world since they had never traveled and weren't content to live under their father's roof for the rest of their lives. Uriah felt he had no choice but to bequeath the house and property to his remaining son to insure that the lineage would be carried on. The Edwards Empire meant *everything* to Uriah."

"And did Dorian carry on the Edwards Empire?"

"It's still a mystery. You see, his disappearance is what caused me to remember what I'd read about those two murders that were similar. Dorian disappeared over fifty years ago."

"He disappeared? Maybe he just up and walked out. Men do such things."

"Yes, men do such things, but I think something must have happened to him. He had two young sons, and as far as anyone who knew him at the time was concerned, he would have never left those boys, that house, or that property. They were all too valuable in the first place, and in the second place, Dorian Edwards gave the appearance that he was a very happy and successful man."

"You have my attention, Hope. I think anytime there are unsolved murders, there is the distinct possibility they may be connected. I have proved that theory on several occasions."

"That's why I'm telling you all this, Jillian. It may be a coincidence, but then again, there may be some connection."

"Tell me, where exactly is this house where Dorian is said to have lived?"

"That's another mystery. Uriah built it so secluded that there isn't even a county record of it. He never filed for permits, and built it with migrant labor, so all we know is what is recorded in his log.

"Since you said Dorian was married, surely there are records that would say where they lived."

She led me to her office and pulled out a file from her cabinet.

"Unfortunately, the records for that period went up in

smoke during one of many fires that were common at that time. However, I've done some research for the museum and come up with some things of interest," she said. "Take a seat, Jillian. I only have a few minutes before I have to get back to the nursery, but I think this won't take long."

I sat down on a captain's chair and waited for her to show me the file.

"What we know from the family Bible is that Dorian married Elsa Jacobs in 1944. They were married for eight years, and then, after a childless marriage, Elsa died, prematurely. About a year before she died, she brought the logs and some artifacts from Uriah and Rebecca that she found in the basement after their deaths, and established this museum, to honor the Edwards family. Then, shortly after Elsa's death, Dorian remarried a woman named Kate Vaughn in 1953. He disappeared in 1961, leaving two sons born by Kate—Phillip, born in 1953, and Virgil, born in 1955. We have school records for the boys until, ironically, 1961."

"That's an amazing coincidence, don't you think?" I asked.

"Coincidence? It's a complete mystery. Anyway, here's the file if you want to take it with you. I'm sure there may be more in it than I've told you. I'm sorry to have to run, but my plants are calling."

"No one understands that better than I do, Hope. Thanks for all the interesting information. I don't have any idea if any of this will all tie in together or not, but I'm sure Detective Montoya would be interested in taking a look at it."

"He's welcome to it. I would like it returned when he's finished with it, though, since it belongs to the museum. Thanks for stopping by, Jillian."

We stepped out into the sunshine, and Hope returned to the nursery. I needed a cup of tea.

7

I got into the car, rolled down the window, and called Walter.

"It's me," I said when he answered.

"I was just going to call you. Where are you right now?" he asked.

"I'm in Canyon Grove. I just finished having an interesting conversation with an old friend of mine, and I'm going to have a cup of tea. Is there any news of the girl?"

"You must have read my mind. I'm afraid she didn't make it. I just got the call from the hospital. You know that this means her death may be a homicide now."

"Because of the car I saw chasing her?"

"Right, it means someone else may have been at fault. Even though we know she hit the deer, it was light enough for her to have seen it. How is Luke doing?"

"I was just about to call and check on him. Should I tell him about the girl, what was her name again?"

"It was Madison Sanders. She was a seventeen-year old senior from Canyon Grove. Her parents said she attended high school over in Clover Hills. I'll check out both schools and see if anyone has missed class. It may cross check with Luke. I think that under the circumstances, we should wait until Luke is stable before telling him his friend is dead."

"I agree. He's still fragile, and it might do more damage than good. Still no word from Frank on any missing persons?"

"I talked to him this morning, and no one's called. Surely, someone must miss a kid like that. He seems so innocent and polite."

"Yeah, like he's been well brought up," I mused. "I think it's very strange, too, Walter. I want to talk to Madison's parents and see if they know anything about Luke. You said they ran a boarding stable?"

"I got the name. It's probably a good idea to pay them a visit. Just look up Sanders Boarding Stables. Listen, Jillian, I have another call coming in. I'm still checking out this Quentin Graves. So far, he only has a record for physical abuse complaints from a couple of women. I'm going to talk to Mary Stewart this afternoon. I'll call you if I find out anything, I promise."

"Thanks, Walter."

I called Cecilia and told her I was going to have a cup tea before I headed home. She said everything was quiet — Luke was asleep with Teddy, and Nurse Turner was at her post in the hall. I told her I'd be home in about an hour.

The Canyon Grove Jazz Café looked like the most likely place to find a cup of tea, so that's where I headed. I parked in front of the long wooden structure that held the few business establishments, and went inside.

A couple of patrons sat at a table against the wall,

watching me as I came in.

"May I help you?" a friendly woman behind the counter asked. Although past her first blush of youth, the woman was still attractive, and had a confident air about her.

"I'd like a cup of tea, please, regular is fine," I said, sitting down at a table in front of a large picture window, facing the street.

"Here you go, ma'am," the woman said, placing the steaming cup of tea before me. "How about some pie or a piece of cake to go with it?" she asked.

"I think just the tea will be fine, thank you." I could tell the other patrons were looking at me, wondering what I was doing there. They looked like locals who probably came here every day to catch up on what was going on in town.

The woman asked, "Did you hear about the murder down at the Mercantile?"

"Yes, I did. Did you know him?"

"I knew him. His name was Quentin Graves. He was a regular who used to come in sometimes for coffee, sometimes for a bite to eat. He always tipped well, I remember that."

"What was he like?"

"He was friendly — sometimes he flirted, which I never minded. I never saw a wedding ring, so I thought it was okay."

"Did he come in alone?"

"Sometimes, but he was usually with another guy. I used to tell my workers, 'Here come the suits.'"

"And you don't know who they worked for?"

"No, not really — we try to get a little familiar with our customers, so they'll come back, but I remember casually asking if they worked around here, you know, just making small talk, and Quentin said, 'We're in sales.' I remember him saying that, because he said it almost like it was an inside joke."

"An inside joke?"

"Yeah, after that I didn't ask. I thought it was strange. Like I said, he came in sometimes for something to drink. I don't know if he lived around here or what, but I had seen him before."

"Maybe he was a rancher...."

"I don't think so. He always wore a suit. Ranchers around here wear working clothes."

"You might be right. What kind of business people do you service?" I probed.

"People like you," she smiled. "What brings you here?"

"I had business over at LaBelle's. I'm sure you must know Verity and Hope."

"I've known them for years. I've lived here all my life. I think I know everyone who lives here. It's a very small community, you know," she said, coming over to my table and checking my tea.

"My name is Jillian Bradley," I said, offering my hand.

"And I'm Iris Young. It's nice to meet you. I own the café. We do most of our business on the weekends here when the tourists come over from Clover Hills to hear the jazz. You should come and have dinner sometime—I think you'd really like it. We're usually packed."

"I was thinking about it when I first saw your sign. This is actually my first time in Canyon Grove. I usually only make it as far as the nursery, and then I head home again."

"It's quiet most of the time, except for this morning. We had police all over the place, and I think every person who lives here was over at the Mercantile trying to get a look at the body. More tea, Jillian?"

"No, thanks, I really need to get home. Tell me, how far is the Sanders Boarding Stables from here?"

"Sanders? It's a couple of miles up the road on the right. You can't miss it. Just keep going up Main Street and turn on Kearny Woods Road — you'll see the sign. Are you going to do some riding?"

"I may, I just wanted to check it out," I said, thinking that may not be such a bad idea. I hadn't been riding since I was a young girl, babysitting for a family on vacation in Squaw Valley.

"Their daughter was just in a car wreck over on Benito Canyon Road the other day. Someone just told me she died a little while ago."

"I'm sorry to hear that. I'll be sure and convey my condolences. Thanks for the tea, how much do I owe you?" She wrote up the ticket and handed it to me.

"Thanks for coming in," she said, "I hope we'll see you again." I paid the bill and walked out of the café, still feeling the eyes of the café patrons upon me.

I decided to find out exactly where the Sanders Boarding Stable was, and ventured up Main Street. I passed a small elementary school, where school had just let out, and yellow buses were lined up ready to take the kids home. There was a small neighborhood behind the school, consisting of a few older homes, and a few older homes on the left hand side of the street, as well. Except for the museum and church, there were no other businesses in town.

Just as Iris had told me, it was only a couple of miles until I saw Kearny Woods Road. I turned right and saw a small sign on the right-hand side with an arrow, indicating that the Sanders Ranch was five miles ahead. It was a beautiful drive through the golden hills, dotted with giant oak trees, their massive canopies silhouetted against the sky. The farther I drove, the more dense the trees grew, until I came to a small clearing just up ahead. A barely visible road on the right led to the Sanders Ranch and Boarding Stables, with the name Sanders spelled out on a wrought iron arch over the entrance. I didn't have enough time to pay a visit, so I drove past the property and looked for a place up ahead where I could turn around safely. The road was narrow, and barely had enough room for two-way traffic. I kept driving for several minutes, until I found a dirt turnoff that looked like a place where I could turn around. There were no signs for the road, so I assumed it was used solely by its owner. On both sides stood heavy woods, and I could see up ahead, that the road turned to the right. I stopped, rolled down my window, and just breathed in the cool, fresh air. I thought I heard the faint trickle of a creek somewhere nearby, and was curious to see where it came from. It won't hurt to drive a little farther, I thought—there might even be a better place to turn around.

I followed the road to the right and noticed it began to incline. The road curved several times and continued to climb. I looked behind in my rear view mirror and saw only woods. Kearny Woods Road was no longer in view. I glanced at the clock in my car, and noticed it was four o'clock. It would be getting dark soon, and I knew I should turn around and go home, but I couldn't. I must have driven for a couple of miles, because the next time I looked at the clock, it said 4:15 p.m.

"This is getting ridiculous!" I said, aloud. "There must be a place to turn around up here." I was almost to the top of the hill when I saw that the road ended at an overlook. I could finally turn around! But how strange for a road to just end like this. I parked, put the parking brake on, just in case, and got out of the car to look around.

The view was breathtaking! I could see for miles around in every direction—cars traveling back and forth down major thoroughfares, the Canyon Grove Water Tower, and a few ranches here and there. I kept looking around, enjoying the view, when I thought I saw a few lights come on through the trees, down in the valley to my right. Could that must be where the owners of this road live, I wondered.

It was growing dark. I knew I needed to start back, but I wanted to find the road that led to that house. I got back into my car, made the turn around, and began searching for a road. I drove along slowly, not seeing anything at first, but then I noticed a lone pine tree growing behind a large boulder. I checked to see if there was a road next to it. My instincts were correct. There it was—a single-lane, dirt road that led down into the valley, and I'm sure it led to the lights of that house.

I drove back down the lonely road, turning on my lights so I could see in the dusk of evening, until I came to Kearny Woods Road. I looked around for a landmark, and found what I was looking for, directly in front of me. A withered old oak tree stood directly across the street. It looked like a hangman's tree, and I knew I wouldn't forget it.

It took almost another hour to get home, due to the rush hour traffic, but I finally made it. I paused for a moment in front of my house to admire my beautiful Christmas tree in the front window, and then turned into my driveway.

"Cecilia, I'm home," I called. Teddy came running when he heard my voice and yipped, until I scooped him up into my arms.

"Verity asked where you were today. She missed seeing you!"

Teddy made a short growl, indicating his recognition of Verity's name. I gave him a hug and a kiss on top of his sweet little head, and then carried him into the living room, where Cecilia had started the fire. I sat down on the sofa, and she sat in the recliner.

"You finally made it home, I see," she said. "Is everything all right?"

"Oh, I'm fine, I almost got lost in the hills, but I found my way back."

Cecilia looked puzzled.

"What were you doing in the hills?"

"I was checking out where the Sanders Boarding Stables were and couldn't turn around, and I wound up on a side road. It's all right now — I'm home. How is Luke doing?"

"He's resting upstairs, and being a good patient. Amanda says it's been quiet all afternoon."

"I'm sure this morning was exhausting for him, having that microchip removed, and all. Are you hungry? I thought I'd order pizza tonight. I'm sure Luke would like it — most teenagers do."

Teddy yipped in favor of my suggestion.

"I'm telling you, Cecilia, that dog knows exactly what I'm saying!" She laughed, and he jumped up into my lap.

Nurse Turner entered the room, and we turned our attention toward her.

"Excuse me Mrs. Bradley, but Luke is awake, and has asked to see you."

"I'll be right up, would you like some pizza? I'm going to order some for dinner tonight," I offered.

"Why, thank you. I will have a piece or two — it will save me some time after I get off work tonight. I'm going to visit my brother over in Canyon Grove."

Cecilia said, "Jillian, would you like me to order it? I have a coupon, and you can visit with Luke if you want."

"I would appreciate that, thanks. I'll go see him now — come along, Teddy." Nurse Turner followed me back up the stairs and waited outside the door, after I knocked, and Luke invited me to come in.

"Hello, Jillian," he said, groggily. He looked out his

window. "It's dark all ready. I must have been asleep a long time."

"Yes, you have been, but that's what Dr. Peters said you need to do, if you're going to get well." Teddy pawed the edge of Luke's bed, indicating he wanted to be where the center of attention was. I picked him up and placed him next to Luke.

"How do you feel?"

"My shoulder is sore, and I can still feel where I hit my head, but I'm okay, thanks for asking."

"I'm ordering a pizza for dinner tonight—does that sound good to you?"

"You're ordering it? They're going to bring it to your house?" he asked.

Never had I seen a young man question with such childlike innocence.

"You mean to tell me you've never had a pizza delivered to your house before?"

"I never knew you could. How can I remember that I've never had a pizza delivered, if I can't remember who I am?"

"Your memory is coming back slowly, I think. You'll remember older events that have happened, before ones that are more recent. Dr. Peters also told me you would still have all your sensory memories. The hardest part will be putting faces to the events that you'll remember."

"It's funny, I know I've eaten pizza before, but I can't remember where I've eaten it."

"Well, try not to think about it too hard, it's not that important. There is one thing I want to ask you about, though."

"Sure, anything, Jillian."

"The first thing you said when you were talking in your sleep was 'He got the stick. He got it.' Does that mean anything to you?"

"He got the stick. He got it." Luke repeated the phrase, and tried to think what it meant. "Nothing comes to mind, Jillian. What would a stick have to do with anything?"

"I really don't know, unless someone got a stick to use to hit something with, or maybe they were caught somewhere and reached for a stick someone was holding out for a rescue of some kind—It could mean several things, I suppose."

"I'll think about it and let you know if I can remember anything," he promised.

"The pizza will be here shortly. I need to wash up and get Teddy's dinner ready, so I'll leave you for a few minutes, but I'll be back."

"Okay, I'll see you in a few minutes."

"Come on, Teddy—let's go get you some dinner."

$$\text{❧ 8 ❧}$$

Nurse Evans took over the night shift from Nurse Turner, and settled Luke in for the night. He had thoroughly enjoyed the novelty of having a pizza delivered—it was truly a first for him. Perhaps his parents were too poor to afford such a treat, or maybe delivery just wasn't available where they lived. Walter was coming over to be with Cecilia for a few minutes, so we sat by the fire, drinking a cup of tea while we waited for him.

The doorbell rang, and Cecilia rose to answer it. "I'll get it, Jillian, you finish your tea."

"Thanks, it's probably Walter."

He strode into the room wearily, arm in arm with Cecilia.

"You look exhausted—sit down before you fall over!" I insisted, pointing to the recliner. "Put your feet up."

"I'll get him a cup of tea, Jillian."

"Thanks, sweetheart, that sounds great right now. I've

been all over the place today."

Cecilia started to go into the kitchen to make the tea, but stopped and turned to Walter, "Now, don't say a word about anything until I get back — I want to hear everything, darling."

"All right, I'll wait, I promise," he said. She left and went to make the tea.

"We're making it in the microwave by the cup tonight, so it won't take long. We've all had a very long day," I said.

Cecilia brought Walter his cup of tea, made just the way he liked it, and sat down to join us.

"Tell us what happened today, sweetheart," she said, as we both gave him our full attention.

"To begin with, we haven't found out anything about Luke's identity. No missing person's reports, nothing on the background check, no identification papers at the crash site, and Madison's parents said she never mentioned anyone fitting his description. I even checked the schools, and came up with nothing. So, all we know, besides his being injected with a microchip, is his blood type is AB positive, he's connected to Madison Sanders somehow, and he seems like a very nice young man."

I had to add, "And he's never heard of pizza delivery before tonight."

"You think that may have significance, Jillian?" Walter asked.

"It may or may not — it just struck me as odd. It could be that he lives too far out. I know they have very specific areas for delivery. I'm sorry to interrupt you, please go on."

Walter sipped his tea and pushed his chair back, hoisting his tired feet into the air.

"The lab is working on finding the source of the chip. They said it could take a day or two, but they'll call me when they have the information. The forensics lab is doing tests on what's left of the car, to determine its make and model, but again, it may take a few days. Jillian, did you get a look at those men leaving the scene of the accident, or a description of their car by any chance?"

I took a sip of tea, and carefully set the cup on top of the coffee table. I tried picturing them in my mind, but I was too far away to get a look at their faces.

"I only remember that the driver was older and a bit bald—he was also a little overweight. The passenger was shorter, and I would say had a stocky build. He was either very tanned, or might have been Hispanic, or East Indian."

No longer able to relax, Walter sat upright after I gave him the description.

"If I showed you a picture, do you think you could make an identification?" Walter asked.

"I might be able to, but I was very far away. I don't know if it would hold up in court."

Cecilia asked, "What about the car?"

"All I remember was that it was black, and I think it must have been expensive…."

"What makes you say that?" Walter asked.

"Because it was so new looking—I've been looking at new cars lately, so when I saw it pull out in front of me, the first thing I thought was, why would someone recklessly drive a new car like that? Listen you two—I'm tired, so I think I'll turn in. Walter, stay as long as you like."

"Don't worry, Jillian," Cecilia said, "I'll lock up and put things away. You get some rest. I'll see you in the morning."

She stood, and gave me a hug and kiss on the cheek goodnight.

"There's just one more thing, Walter. Did you have a chance to talk to Mary Stewart this afternoon?"

"I did. She was very closed about him, I thought. When she talked, she kept looking at the door, as if she expected someone to burst in. I think she was afraid of someone, or something."

"I think I would be, too, after what happened. Did you learn anything else about Quentin?"

"A little. She told me he was quite a regular for the jazz nights. He smiled at her and her husband, as if he acknowledged they were both regular aficionados. She also mentioned that he was usually with another man when he came in. She only saw him with a woman once or twice."

"I wonder if that was Nurse Turner's friend that she mentioned."

"It could have been. I asked her what he was like. She told me he seemed quite jovial, but not obtrusive in any way. She said she really thought he was just a local business man."

"So he didn't seem fearful of anyone, is that what you mean?"

"That's the impression I got."

"So, she must be wary because he was murdered."

"Wouldn't you be?"

"Yes, I think I would."

"I'm going to bed now, you two. Keep your seat, Walter," I said, when he started to get up.

He blew me a kiss goodnight.

"I'll talk to you both tomorrow."

I stopped in the hall, where I had laid the file Hope had given me, and carried it to my room. Cecilia would stay upstairs in the room next to Luke, making sure someone familiar would be available, in case he needed anything during the night. "Come along, Teddy, let's go to bed, it's been a very long day."

I ran a hot bath, added lots of bubble bath, tucked my hair up in a clip, and stepped into the fragrant water. I sank beneath the water up to my neck, and let my body float in the warmth. I could only relax for a few minutes, because my mind kept wandering to the file. Hope had told me I would find more. I wondered if she knew something that could tie into Quentin Grave's murder. It was as if she wanted me to be the one to find it, and not her. Maybe I would understand what it was when I found it.

I finished my bath and got ready for bed as quickly as I could, placing Teddy on his towel at the foot of my bed. I crawled in between the covers, propped myself up on my pillows, and switched on the overhead reading light with my remote.

Teddy began to softly growl. The growl rose in volume, and I knew he was on the alert. He didn't move, but just kept growling, turning slowly, and looking toward the window.

"What's the matter, boy? Do you hear someone outside?"

Teddy paused for a moment, and then looked at me with his soft brown eyes, full of concern. Although he didn't move from his towel, he had told me that someone was out there, and it was someone who was not a friend.

Since he seemed calm again, I assumed the possible intruder had left, and was no longer a threat. "You're a good dog, Teddy, and I love you." I stroked his head and back, gave him a kiss goodnight, and then returned to looking at the file.

Hope had organized the file into three sections: The first was labeled, "Uriah and Rebecca Edwards"; the second was, "Dorian and Elsa Edwards"; and the third was, "Dorian and Kate Edwards, Phillip, and Virgil." I glanced at the clock, which said 9:10 p.m., and promised myself to go to sleep in an hour. After reading the whole file, the clock said midnight. I reassembled the papers and set them on my nightstand, as Teddy twitched in his sleep, dreaming of the things dogs dream of, letting out a tiny whimper here and there.

I turned off the light and pulled the covers up to my neck, still thinking about all the facts I had read. "Lord," I prayed, "please help me find Luke's family, and if there's anything You want me to see from reading this file, please open my eyes."

I was tired, but not sleepy. The most disturbing fact I had read about was the county sheriff's account in 1911. That account stated that the bodies of the two migrant workers were found on the ground in front of the mercantile barn. I was beginning to see Hope's point of the similarities between the murder incidents, past and present. I continued processing what I had read about the Edwards men, Uriah and Dorian, and I considered what type of person would want to live so distant from everyone. Uriah was a pioneer of sorts, who had followed his father's example of being a rancher. Dorian had obviously done the same thing. Both were successful, and happily married, even though Dorian had no offspring by his first wife.

According to the records, Uriah and Rebecca were living with Dorian and Elsa up until the time of their deaths, which must have been stressful for Dorian, having to live up to his father's omnipresence of success at all times. Elsa must have felt like a goldfish in a bowl, and under the scrutiny of Rebecca, as well. For all intents and purposes, it was not a normal household situation. If I had been Elsa, I would have wanted to get rid of my in-law's things after they were dead, too, so I would feel like my own life could finally begin. Creating a memorial like the museum was a brilliant idea on her part. But why not just toss them away? It was as though Elsa wanted someone to find out about Uriah's unlawful dealings, and that's why she passed the information to the public.

The Edwards family was self-sufficient, for the most part, growing their food, or raising it. They had vast gardens, orchards, and a slaughterhouse, and only had to bring in flour, sugar, and spices from the outside world. A large plumbing system was put in to accommodate their watering needs, and the house was fully run on electricity from a generator on the property that Uriah had installed. I learned that the women stayed at home and oversaw the cooking and laundry, while the men would go into town, and bring back anything they needed. The women made their own clothes, and seemed to be content, sitting outside in the garden after dinner in the summertime, or in front of the fireplace in the wintertime. It seemed that for the wives, it was a world unto themselves, and for the men, who knows what they did whenever they left the property, sometimes for several days at a time…. I would think more about it tomorrow, but for now, I would get a good night's sleep.

The next morning I awoke early, refreshed, and ready for the day. At the end of my bed, Teddy stretched, and wagged his tail, happy to wish me a good morning. I picked him up, and hugged him to me, giving him my usual kiss on top of his sweet little head. I dressed quickly, made my bed, and opened all the shutters in the house. I let Teddy out into the back yard for his morning constitution, while I made coffee. The upstairs seemed quiet. I'll let them sleep while I check my computer, I thought.

First, I checked my e-mails, deleting most of them, then Facebook, and then my bank account. After I'd finished catching up with everyone and everything, I finally went to my webpage. I found several comments and questions for my column that I would need to address after breakfast. Teddy barked, telling me that he was ready to come in, so I poured a cup of coffee, went to the conservatory, and opened the back door.

Sunshine filled the room, and I sat down on my rattan sofa to bask in its warmth. I knew Teddy would be wanting a bit of breakfast by now, but I sat enjoying my first cup of coffee, looking at my paintings that I had purchased over the years. I especially enjoyed the modern, yellow diptychs that I had purchased in Scottsdale on my last trip. There was a brief moment when I was reminded about a dear man I had met at that time, but I pushed it from my mind. That was over. I knew I had to move on.

After finishing my coffee, and at the insistence of Teddy, I went to the kitchen to make breakfast for everyone. I could hear water starting to flow through the pipes, and knew Cecilia would be down soon. Nurse Turner arrived to relieve Nurse Evans, and said she would go and check on Luke, and get him ready for breakfast.

Cecilia came into the kitchen, dressed for the day in a mustard-yellow turtleneck, jeans, and silver hoop earrings. The outfit was becoming to her long auburn hair, and slim figure.

She smiled.

"Good morning, Jillian, how did you sleep last night?"

"Very well, thank you, how about you?"

"I slept soundly, thanks. I didn't hear anything from Luke, so I assume he slept through the night."

"Coffee?" I offered, bringing the pot over to the table where she sat.

"Thank you, I would love some. What are you planning to do today?"

"Well, after I take Luke some breakfast and touch bases with him, I think I'd like to check out the Sanders Boarding Stables to see if I can learn anything. I saw something when I was trying to turn around yesterday that I'd like to check out."

Cecilia put her toast down. There was a look of concern on her face.

"You're not going by yourself, are you?"

I shrugged my shoulders.

"I had thought about it. I think the Sanders might open up to me, if they think I'm just a client."

"Jillian, I don't think you should take any chances. Can't you get someone to come with you — what about Ann, or Nicole?"

"I suppose I could ask one of them. Ann might be game for a horseback ride. All right, I'll call her right now."

After calling Ann, who graciously agreed to come with me, I made an appointment for the ride, then took Luke his breakfast. It was my specialty — eggs over easy on buttered toast, sprinkled with salt, pepper, grated cheddar cheese, and just a light sprinkle of Lawry's Seasoned Salt.

Luke was sitting up in bed, looking rested.

"Good morning," he said. Teddy, who always follows the food, ran to him, and yipped once, asking to be put on the bed.

"Good morning, Teddy. Nurse, would you hand him to me please?"

She scooped him up and put him on the bed next to Luke. Teddy licked his face, and wagged his tail as Luke pet him. I placed the tray across his lap, and asked how he was feeling.

"I feel better this morning. Nurse said I slept through the night — I guess I didn't talk in my sleep."

"I'm glad you're feeling better. I have to go out later this morning on an errand, but Nurse Turner and Cecilia will be here to make sure you rest, and have what you need. I may not be back until this afternoon, but just know that I'm going on your behalf trying to find out who you are. What would you like for dinner tonight?"

"Chicken and Dumplings, and mashed potatoes sound good. Do you know how to make them?" he asked innocently, as if he ate them often.

I was a little taken back.

"I do know how to make them, but I also need a full day to prepare them! Maybe I'll make them for you when I'm home all day." Maybe his mother doesn't have a job outside the home, and spends all day cooking, I thought.

"That's okay," he said, looking out the window for a brief moment. "How about fried chicken, greens, and cornbread? I like that, too."

"Now *that*, I might be able to come up with—I'll see what I can do. Now eat your breakfast, and take your pills so you can get some good rest today. I'll check in on you before I go, I promise."

"Thank you, Jillian. By the way, I do remember something, something about what I said the night before about the stick."

"What is it?"

"I think I have a dog. I remember throwing him a stick, and saying those words. It felt like I was very young at the time."

"That's a good sign that your memory may be returning. Could you see what the dog looked like?"

"I couldn't see his face, but I don't think he was small, like Teddy, he was much bigger."

"Perhaps if you were small, he could have seemed large, I suppose. Anyway, it's something, and I think it's a good sign that you *are* going to find out where you belong."

"You think so?"

Luke's face was expectant.

"Yes, I do. Now you finish your breakfast. I'll be back up soon. Teddy, stay here with Luke, and be a good dog." Teddy yipped that he understood the command with no trouble at all. What an intelligent dog he is, I thought with pride.

Cecilia was finishing the dishes when I returned downstairs.

"Cecilia, dear, I have a file I want Walter to look at, so when you see him today, please give it to him."

"Sure, just set it on the dining room table so I won't forget to give it to him. He said he should know today what the lab has to say about that victim over in Canyon Grove. I'm sure he'll want to touch bases with you sometime today."

"I hope to be back in time to get dinner on. I promised Luke I would have fried chicken, greens, and cornbread."

Cecilia's eyebrows shot up in surprise.

"That's an interesting menu — how are you going to do all that in such a short time?"

I grinned.

"Never fear — there's fried chicken take out, and canned greens, and cornbread mixes at the grocery store. No problem, I'll bring it all home with me after my ride."

"You're too much. Now *I'm* looking forward to dinner!"

❧9❧

Dressed in jeans, long-sleeved shirt, and boots, I met Ann in front of the Jazz Café in Canyon Grove. She was already waiting for me, as usual. After joining me in my car, we started up Main Street, passing the school and small neighborhood, and turned off on Kearny Woods Road.

Ann smiled, and turned her head toward me as I drove.

"Care to share with the class?" she asked.

I explained the events of the past two days, and she didn't say one word until I'd finished the whole story.

"That's quite a story, Jillian. You've taken in a stray, and now you're determined to find out who he is. So, am I to understand that this ride today is a fact finding mission

I smiled and answered, "That's exactly what it is. You see, Madison was the last person Luke was in contact with, and I believe there has to be some link to help us find out who he is."

"Even though she's dead?" she replied.

Ann stared out the window.

"I don't know, Jillian, it sounds far-fetched to me."

"Well, it's all we have right now, Ann."

The sign for the Sander's Ranch came up on the right, and I drove by it.

Ann looked perplexed.

"Where are you going, Jillian? You passed it!"

"I know. I want to show you something before we take this ride."

I found the hanging tree, and turned right, onto the dirt road I had driven on before. I showed her the overlook, and pointed to the location where I had seen the lights in the stand of oaks below. I showed her the road that I believe led to the structure, whatever it was.

"When we go on our ride, I want to be on the lookout for that place down there. It can't be that far away from the Sander's Ranch."

"All right," she said, nodding her head, "why don't we make a note on your GPS, so we'll have an idea where we are right now?"

"Then we'll figure the mileage and direction back to the Sander's, and the timing we can figure out later. I knew you would come in handy, Ann. I also brought along my compass in case we get lost. All these hills look alike to me. Are you ready to ride?"

"Let's do it!"

We carefully took note of our position, and drove back to the ranch, marking the distance, direction, and time it took. Now all we had to do was figure out how fast the horse would travel. It wasn't going to be easy.

The Sander's Ranch was modest, but very well kept. Since no one was outside when we arrived, we walked over to the house, which stood behind the barn, and knocked on the door.

No one answered at first, and I had to remind myself that these were grieving parents. The door slowly opened, and Mrs. Sanders asked if we had made the appointment for the ride. Her face looked weary and haggard from grief.

"Please come in ladies," she offered. "My husband is getting everything ready for you. I apologize for not being ready but...."

"Mrs. Sanders," I said, "please sit down, we're in no hurry, and we understand what you've just gone through."

She thanked us and cried a little, but soon composed herself.

The house was simply furnished in a country western style, and there were pictures of Madison everywhere – on the fireplace mantle, on the end table, and on top of the old upright piano.

"That was Madison's senior picture," Mrs. Sanders said when she saw my gaze. "We've only had it a week. She would have graduated this year but now...," and once again, Madison's mother broke down in tears.

"She was a beautiful girl. I'm sure you were very proud of her."

I decided to be direct, since Mr. Sanders would soon be ready for us to take our ride.

"Mrs. Sanders, I understand that Madison had a boy in the car with her. Did you know who he was?"

Her face contorted with pain, as if I had physically injured her.

"Why is everyone asking me about this boy? We have no idea who he was, or what he was doing with our daughter. But, I'll tell you this, we trusted Madison. She was a good girl, and we raised her with good moral values. Whatever he was doing in her car, there was a good reason, that's all I know – she was a good girl!

"Please excuse me," she said, calming herself. "I didn't

mean to get so upset, I apologize."

"There's no apology necessary," I said, gently. "You said everyone is asking you about the boy? Can you tell me who?"

"I think that's what I'm so upset about. You see, the man who came asking about the boy was found murdered. What is *happening*? I don't understand any of it."

The front door opened, and Mr. Sanders told us our mounts were ready. Seeing his wife so upset, he looked to us for an explanation.

"We were just offering our condolences, Mr. Sanders," I said. "We're very sorry about losing your daughter."

"Thank you, ma'am."

"I think we're ready for that ride now," Ann said, coming to my aide.

Mr. Sanders was a man of few words. He looked like he had been a rancher all of his life, by the way he walked and carried himself.

"Have you ladies ever ridden a horse before?" he asked in an expressionless tone of voice.

"I've ridden a few times," said Ann.

"I have too," I said, confidently.

"All right then," said Mr. Sanders, handing us brochures.

"There are a few choices of trails you can take. Whatever you do, stay on the path, and as soon as you've gone halfway on the time you want to ride, turn around, and head home. Any questions?"

"I have one," Ann said. "How fast do these horses go?"

Mr. Sanders looked at her, as if she might not be all there, but answered the question as seriously as he could.

"That horse, ma'am, can go up to 30 MPH. A walk is about 2-4 MPH; a trot is 8-10 MPH; a cantor or lope is 10-17 MPH; and a gallop, which is all these horses can do, is 30

MPH. Any other questions?"

"No, thank you, we'll be back in about two hours, and if not, you'd better come looking for us," I laughed.

Mr. Sanders did not laugh.

Ann looked at her watch, and we began our ride with a walk.

It was a fine day for a ride. The sun had warmed the air considerably, and as we ventured forth, a few birds called to each other from the trees. Occasionally, we spotted a few cattle sunning themselves on nearby hills, as hawks and buzzards flew lazily overhead against a blue sky, punctuated with wisps of cirrus clouds. We picked up the pace a bit. The horses seemed to enjoy galloping more than sauntering, and we were able to keep up the pace for a while, until I felt we needed to check our position.

The brochures were marked for distance in quarter mile increments, and markers were unobtrusively placed along the path which ran along a narrow creek. I used the compass to check our direction, and with Ann's brilliant calculations, we wound up in the middle of nowhere. According to the last marker, we had been gone thirty minutes, and couldn't see anything but hills and oak-studded grasslands. We stopped our horses and reconnoitered, trying to figure out where we were, in conjunction to the overlook we had been on before.

"Ann, I think we're lost."

"Maybe, but I think we should ride up to the top of that hill, and see if we can tell where we are. We don't have much time until we have to turn around."

"Let's go then."

Our steeds had no trouble climbing up to the top of the hill. Once we had reached the top, we dismounted and surveyed our position. We could see the creek, and figured out how to get back to the path.

"According to my compass, that overlook we were on should be right over there," I pointed.

Ann looked through the binoculars she had brought with her, then looked to where I was pointing.

"I think I see it! Take a look." She handed me the binoculars.

I looked, and knew it must be the same place. The area looked as if someone had cleared it for a viewing point.

"So," I said, "according to our calculations, those lights should be coming from somewhere …."

Ann touched my arm.

"Jillian, look over there, just to the left of those two giant oaks. I thought I saw some reflections of some kind. Do you see them?" she asked, pointing down to the stand of oaks below. I raised the binoculars, then looked to where she was pointing.

"I see it. It looks like the back of a large house. There's a huge garden up next to it, and several out buildings I can make out. I bet those reflections are bits of metal that people put in their gardens, to scare off the birds."

Ann said, "Let me have a look." I handed her the binoculars, and she put them up to her eyes. "Now that's something you don't see every day."

I had to agree.

"It almost looks like a compound of some kind, and it looks as if whoever lives there, wants to be left alone. I don't think anyone would notice it was even there, unless someone stood right here and did what we did. I don't even see a road leading in or out of the property. It must be hidden by more trees."

"Why are you so curious about that house down there, Jillian?"

"Hope LaBelle gave me a file to read about the Edwards family that used to live around here. She believed, and the file supports her theories, that the family heads were corrupt enough to carry out murder. She feels that the recent murder might tie in somehow. The last case involved a man named Dorian Edwards, who disappeared fifty years ago. That was the last recollection anyone has had of the Edwards family. I saw a picture of the house in the museum that Hope says no one knows the exact location of, and I think I would recognize it if I saw it. However, I would have to see the front of it. I believe it has to be checked out. Nothing else points to where Luke comes from, or I think we would have heard something by now. I also have an idea of how to get inside, if you'll help me fix these coordinates."

"Sure, I think we'd better get started back since it's been an hour."

Ann wrote down the coordinates on the brochure, so we could find the house again. We mounted our steeds, and rode back to the stables. Mr. Sanders was waiting by the corral gate when we returned. He didn't greet us, or even act surprised that we came back right on time. He helped us dismount, then led the horses to the barn, where his wife was waiting.

"She'll take care of your bill," he said. He took the horses into their stalls, and began removing their saddles.

Mrs. Sanders motioned for us to step inside the tiny office, just inside the front door of the barn, and began filing out the invoice. "It's $55 for the ride, and with the tax, that will be $60.09 a piece, ladies," she said. "I hope you enjoyed your ride."

We paid, and took the invoice that she handed to us.

"We had a good ride," I said. "The weather was perfect today."

"It was, wasn't it?" Ann replied.

"Well, we hope you'll come back again sometime. Thank you for your business." Mrs. Sanders closed up the desk and started to walk us out of the office, locking the door behind her.

"By the way," I said, "do you know the people who have the large garden behind their house, a few miles from here? We saw it in the distance, when we were on top of a hill."

Mrs. Sanders looked truly surprised.

"A garden, did you say?"

She shook her head.

"Not that I know of. The closest neighbor we have is Rick Turner, but he doesn't have a garden. He's a bachelor who buys everything in town."

"You said his name is Rick Turner?" I slowed my pace. "Does he by any chance have a sister who is a nurse?" I asked.

"I believe he does. He's a nice man, and a good neighbor. He came by earlier and paid his respects. He doesn't live too far from here—just down the road a little ways. Well, I need to be getting lunch for Bill, if you'll excuse me."

I offered her my card, and told her she could call me, if she felt like talking to someone. I told her I had lost someone very dear to me, as well.

She took the card, and quietly thanked me.

"You've been very kind," she said. "There is something that has bothered us about Madison, and I don't know if it means anything or not, but about a month before all this happened, we noticed that she would go off on a ride by herself."

"Did she do that often?" Ann asked.

"Yes, but she always came home after about an hour. However, for the past month she would go off, and not return for two or three hours. When we asked her where she had been, she was evasive, and would busy herself with homework, or chores."

"How often did this happen? I asked.

"It was only about three or four times, until last Saturday when...." Mrs. Sanders began to break down as she thought of Madison's accident.

I put my arm around her shoulder to comfort her.

"I know this is hard, but what happened last Saturday?"

"After she took off on a ride, her horse returned without her. Her father and I were worried that she may have fallen, and went to look for her, but found nothing. The next thing we heard was that she had been in a car accident, and was in the hospital in critical condition. I just don't understand any of it."

"I know, I don't think anyone does, but I'm sure the police will find out what really happened. A dear friend of mine is handling the case. Would you like me to tell him what you told me? It may help somehow."

Mrs. Sanders bent her head, and nodded her consent. "I suppose it really doesn't matter what the police know now that Madison is gone. You have my permission."

"It may bring closure. I've heard that when you have that, it makes it a little easier to heal," I offered, hoping to help console her.

"Thank you," she said, "By the way, before that man came asking questions, I had never seen him before. At first, I thought he was a detective, but he never showed me a badge. He was very polite, and I thought he might be a private investigator, but he never did say who he worked for, he just asked about Madison's boyfriends. I wish there was something else I could tell you. He seemed so nice. Why would anyone want to kill him?"

"I'm sure we'll find out eventually. Thanks again for talking with us. We enjoyed our ride."

"That's good, I'm glad. Well, I really need to see to Bill, if you'll please excuse me." She walked back into her house, and closed the door slowly, watching us, until we returned to our car and left.

Ann turned to me after we started back to our cars.

"Well, that was sad. I feel sorry for her."

We walked to the car and got in, not saying anything because of the sadness we felt.

After a few moments though, Ann asked, "Are you hungry?"

"As a matter of fact I am. What do you have in mind?"

"Do you want to go somewhere and get some lunch — my treat?"

"That's nice of you. I need to check in with Walter first, if you don't mind. Where sounds good to you — anywhere is fine with me."

"It's such a nice day. I'd like to eat outside."

"I would say the Jazz Café, but I think it's too close to where that grizzly murder happened to be appetizing, don't you think?" I shuddered.

"I agree with you. I saw it when I drove in, and it was horrible, the police were still going over the crime scene. Let's go to that good bakery in Clover Hills. We could have brunch."

"All right, I'll meet you there in a few minutes, it shouldn't take too long."

I dropped Ann off at her car and waved goodbye as she pulled out, then made my call.

"Walter, it's Jillian, I thought I would call and check how you're doing with Luke's case."

"Hi, Jillian, we're running the tests on the paint chip of the car Madison was driving. We'll find out whom it belonged to — it wasn't hers according to her parents."

"Ann and I just came from there. I decided to find out if

they knew anything more than what they told you about Luke."

"You took Ann with you?"

"Well, it was actually Cecilia's idea that I shouldn't go alone. We went for a horseback ride."

"I didn't realize you rode!"

"I don't, really, except I thought it would serve us better if we had a reason to talk to them."

"Did it work?"

"I think it was a very informative trip. We found out that Quentin Graves paid them a visit, asking about Madison's passenger right before he was killed. Mrs. Sanders was upset about that, which I certainly can understand."

"That's quite a coincidence. What else did you find out?"

"She also told us that Madison had taken longer rides than usual, and wouldn't tell them where she went. That sounds to me like rendezvous' of some kind."

"I suppose they could have been. I'll make a note of it, though."

"And there's something else. I don't know if it will come to anything, but we found a hidden compound of some kind when we were on our ride. That's actually the reason we even went on the ride — to see if we could find the source of some lights I saw coming from that area yesterday afternoon. Have you looked at that file I left for you?"

"Yes I did, although it just looks like a bunch of historical data about Canyon Grove. What was I supposed to be looking for?"

"Nothing in particular — I just wanted to see if you saw the account of the county sheriff in 1911, regarding the two bodies found in downtown Canyon Grove."

"I must have missed that little fact. Let's have it, Jillian.

I apologize for not paying better attention."

"I just noted that both of the victims had been badly beaten, and their throats slit—like Quentin Graves. I don't know, it just called to mind a similar type of killing, *meant to punish*."

"Yeah, I can see that. So you think we have a murderer who killed 99 years ago, and is on the loose again?"

"Of course not, but it may be a descendent."

"Jillian, that sounds somewhat far-fetched, but then I don't believe it was a ritual killing either. Quentin Graves had most of his blood still in him."

"Well, I wanted you to see something else. Hope thinks this is a very important fact. Did you happen to notice that Uriah's son Dorian disappeared fifty years' ago?"

"You think Uriah killed his own son?"

"I don't know—it's just interesting that murder may run in that family."

"I suppose it could, but remember, we have to deal in facts, not hearsay. I don't know how many witnesses you could come up with for murders that happened that long ago."

"I understand the difficulty, but you know I'm only trying to do whatever I can to help Luke find out who he is. It breaks my heart to see such a fine young man so lost!"

"I appreciate that, Jillian, and we're going to do everything we can. You mentioned finding a compound of some kind?"

"I think it may be the old Edward's place, which seems to have disappeared in the last few years. I noticed a picture of it in the museum when I was visiting yesterday afternoon. Different people may live there now, but I need to find out. We don't have anything else right now until we find out more about the microchip, and Quentin Graves. Have you found out any more about him?"

"I just got back the report. His background check revealed that he last worked for an agricultural agency called, Hale AgRecruitment, here in Clover Hills. I plan to check it out. And don't forget the car. I'll check on that again in a few minutes. I should also be hearing about the details of that microchip very soon. What are you planning to do now?"

"Ann and I are going to have brunch in Clover Hills, and after that, I'll be checking in with Luke. That compound had a huge garden in the back, so I'm going to pay them a visit to get a story about it for my column. I'll take Teddy with me."

"Be careful, Jillian, I think I'd take Ann with you, too, isn't she an amateur photographer?"

"Yes, she is. That's brilliant, Walter. I'm sure she'd come with me; she said she'd help me if I needed her."

"Good, I sure would feel better if you did, and if you think it feels dangerous, don't take a chance. Just get out of there, promise?"

"I'll be careful, I promise. I have to let you go, we're at the bakery. Take care, Walter, and I'll talk to you soon."

❧10❧

Ann and I enjoyed a lovely brunch at the bakery—it was pleasant sitting on the covered porch, watching people pass by occasionally, walking their dogs, or strolling hand in hand. Such an idyllic town we lived in—I wondered if anyone else had troubles like Luke did. Nurse Evans must have read my thoughts, because she called me right at that moment.

"Sorry to bother you, Jillian, but you said to tell you if Luke remembered anything."

"Yes, of course. What did he remember?"

"He said that he could remember someone crying during the night. He said it sounded like a woman, or a girl, and at first, he thought he might have dreamed it, but he remembered it happening twice, and it sounded the same way."

"Thank you, Amanda. I think you should get him to rest. I'll get home as soon as I can."

Ann said, "So, Luke had another memory?"

"Yes, he did, and it was not a very pleasant one either. I'm afraid his family must be mixed up in something, if he's hearing crying at night. Even if it's someone in his family who's doing the crying—it may mean they're in trouble somehow."

"You're talking about physical abuse?"

"Perhaps, or it may be something worse. Ann, we have to find out what's going on in that house."

When I explained my excursion plans to visit the compound with her as my photographer, she was flattered and consented immediately. She was a true friend indeed to stick her neck out like that with me.

I couldn't resist buying a few decorated Christmas cookies from the bakery. I hadn't made any since I was first married. We paid our bill, and began walking back to our car, when I heard my name being called out.

"Jillian!"

I turned and saw Prentice Duval getting out of his car.

"Hello, Ann," he said in his usual charming voice. "What brings you ladies to town this lovely day?"

"Hello, Prentice," I said, always glad to see this handsome, well-dressed man. "We've just finished brunch. You know, I've been meaning to stop by the gallery to see the Woody Biggs exhibit—I love his work, but I've been so busy with Christmas, and Cecilia's engagement party, that I just haven't had a spare moment."

"I understand how it is. Fortunately, we'll have his works for at least another month, so I hope you can stop by before they're all sold. Everyone thinks he's quite the genius."

Prentice glanced up and down at our riding garb, and asked the question with his eyes.

"We've just been for a horseback ride over in Canyon

Grove."

"Really, I didn't know you rode, Jillian, or you either Ann. If I had known, I would have asked you ladies to come out with me sooner—I was *born* on horseback."

"I never knew that, Prentice. I suppose there are a lot of things I don't know about you," I teased.

"Well, how about dinner Friday night, then. I could fill you in."

"I would love that. Would you like to go over to the Canyon Grove Jazz Café? I hear it's fun, and the food is good."

"I've never been there, but I've always wanted to try it, so I would love to, how about seven o'clock? Ann you're welcome to come with us," he graciously asked, knowing she'd decline.

"Thanks, Prentice, but I've made other plans—you and Jillian go and have a good time."

"Seven is fine with me," I agreed, suddenly anxious to get home. "Prentice, you'll have to excuse us, but I need to get home. I have something I need to take care of. It was lovely seeing you, and I'll look forward to Friday evening. Goodbye!"

Prentice kissed my hand, which made me blush a little, and then turned, and walked away.

"Jillian," Ann said, with a smile curving her lips, "I think you have an admirer."

"He probably admires lots of women, Ann. We're just good friends who like to have dinner together occasionally, and I need to see more of that jazz café in Canyon Grove. It may lead to nothing, but I sure don't think it would hurt to be acquainted with more of the locals. It's one small town. Surely someone knows who Luke is—I just have to find out whom."

Ann smiled at my explanation, and halfway believed it.

"Please stay in touch, Jillian, and let me know when you want to check out that compound. By the way, I enjoyed the ride, even if we did get lost a little. I'll see you later."

Ann walked to her car, and I started walking to mine, which was parked around the corner, and down a side street. I passed several shops, and surveyed my surroundings.

Clover Hills was a small town—not nearly as small as Canyon Grove, but small just the same. As I rounded the corner, I noticed a title company, located on the bottom floor of the old red brick building. Next to it was an insurance business, and then I walked passed Arnie's Steakhouse, where I had eaten several times, and tried to remember when I'd last been there. Across the street was a dress shop, with a few holiday outfits displayed in the window. Next to it was the Red Robin Dairy, a favorite drive-through, where you could order grocery items and ice - cream cones from your car window. It was one of my favorite places to go to, when I needed to get out of the house.

I arrived at my car, and glanced across the street at the office building, occupying the lot next to the dairy. I noticed several signs, indicating various businesses located inside, and one caught my eye in particular. It read, *Hale AgRecruitment Agency.* So that's where Quentin Graves worked before he was murdered. I wondered if Nurse Turner knew his name from this place, I would have to ask her.

I stopped by the mall on the way home, and picked up a few clothes for Luke—I enjoyed buying them, but cautioned my emotions not to become too attached to this young man. I knew he could be gone as quickly as he had come into my life, and I didn't relish the pain of losing someone I cared for again. I had lost my husband years ago, and that was enough pain for a lifetime.

After stopping at the grocery store to pick up the canned greens and cornbread mix, I went through a drive through, and picked up a bucket of fried chicken, sides of corn on the cob, mashed potatoes and gravy, and some biscuits with honey butter.

It was good to be home. As I walked in the kitchen door, Teddy ran to greet me, wagging his tail. He stretched his paws up on my leg, begging to be picked up. I put the sacks of clothes on the counter, and placed the food in the oven, which I turned on to 250 degrees, to keep it warm.

"Come here, sweet little doggie," I gushed. I gave him plenty of hugs and attention before going into the living room, where I knew I would find Cecilia.

She was sitting by the fire, reading the latest issue of *Today's Bride* magazine, and started to stand when I entered, but I insisted she keep her seat. She motioned for me to sit in my recliner, closed the magazine, and set it back on the coffee table.

"I can't get over how expensive wedding gowns are. I've even checked with the consignment shops, and they're still overpriced," she said, discouraged.

"I know how frugal you are. I had to be, too. We didn't have a large budget for our wedding, either. I remember borrowing my neighbor's wedding dress, and having it altered to save money.

"When you think about it, it's not important what kind of a wedding you have. What is important is the kind of marriage you have, and you and Walter will have a great one. There's no doubt about it."

"Thanks, Jillian. That makes me put things into perspective. How was your ride with Ann?"

"I got through it. I'm glad you suggested that she go with me. We had a nice brunch together, afterward."

"I'm glad you could do that. You needed a nice break after these past few days. Luke and I have had a good day, so far. He says he's feeling better, and Nurse Turner is making sure he gets his rest. I made us lunch, and the dishes are finished."

"Thank you, Cecilia, is he awake now?"

"I think he is."

"I think I'll go up and see him, I'll be back in a few minutes."

I scooped up Teddy and ascended the stairs, finding Nurse Turner sitting outside of Luke's room. His door was closed, so I assumed he had fallen asleep again.

"How is he doing, nurse?"

She put her finger to her lips, indicating I should whisper, and answered accordingly.

"He just now dozed off—but he says he's feeling much better."

"I'm so glad to hear it. I need to ask you something. You said you had heard the name Quentin Graves before, but you didn't know where."

She pursed her lips, and screwed up her eyes, slightly.

"Yes, I remember saying that."

"Did you ever have any dealings with the Hale AgRecruitment Agency? Their office is in Clover Hills, next to the dairy."

"Is that the dairy where you get the ice-cream cones at the drive thru?"

"Yes, that's the one."

"Let me think."

She looked to her left for a moment, and whispered, "I remember now—it wasn't the agency, a friend of mine told me about someone she was dating at the time, and I believe that was the man's name. I remember it, because I commented on it sounding like a cross, between San

Quentin and the grave, I told her I didn't like the way it sounded."

"Do you still stay in touch with this friend?"

"On occasion. I still have her number if you would like to get in touch with her."

"I would like to contact her. Does she live in Clover Hills?"

"Yes, she lives over in a condominium close to downtown. I have her number right here in my cell."

Nurse Turner scrolled down her contacts, and I programmed the name and number into my phone.

"Thank you, Amanda. I'll talk to you later. I need to make a phone call."

I went downstairs again and phoned Walter. He was very appreciative of the information Nurse Turner had given me, and said he would give her friend a call.

"Would you like me to go with you?" I offered.

"Absolutely, Jillian, I'll let you know when I can get away. Right now, we're checking on the microchip, and paint samples from the car Madison was driving. I hope to get more information by Wednesday at the latest."

"Well, Luke is feeling better, and that's good. He's slowing regaining his memory. He's mentioned a dog now, so that may be something. The only problem, however, is that it may have been a long time ago, and may not help us. I'm still hoping we can find out more, though. Are you coming over for dinner tonight?"

"That depends on what you're making."

"Luke has asked for fried chicken, greens, and cornbread. I promised I would make it for him. I've already picked up the food—I just need to make the cornbread. You are more than welcome."

"I was just kidding. I had planned to come over to give Cecilia a chance to get out and do some shopping, so you might as well count us in."

I laughed, and said I totally understood. I knew that Cecilia had already said she wanted to have dinner with us, but I also knew she would want all of Walter's attention at some point during the day. Young couples needed that. I understood, and didn't take it personally.

I just had one more thing I wanted to do before taking a break. I sat down to my computer and pulled up Google Earth, placing the notations Ann and I came up with, locating the compound, next to the keyboard. I traced the coordinates to where I thought we had been, and zeroed into the location where that house should be, according to our calculations. I found Kearny Woods Road and traced it to where I thought the turnoff, by the hanging tree, would have been. No road was visible, but I kept searching the area, until I found where the overlook looked like it might be.

After looking at the area for several minutes, I finally found an area that had habitation, and zoomed in. I could barely make it out, but there it was! Surrounded by masses of oak trees, there stood the gabled brick house, with the five chimneys, barely visible, tucked in and around the tree canopies. I could make out the house itself, the large garden plot in the back, what looked like a long garage, a few small outbuildings, and a small structure that looked like another garage or outbuilding of some sort. I bookmarked the page and printed out several copies, so I could give one to Walter, one to Ann, and maybe even one to Luke. I would be very interested to see his reaction to it.

I was so focused on my computer that I didn't hear Luke come in.

"Hi, Jillian," he said. "I couldn't stay in bed any longer. I hope you don't mind me coming down."

He was dressed in his own clothes that I had laundered

for him, but it was the second day he had worn them.

"Not at all, Luke, have a seat here next to me," I said, pointing to the comfortable swivel rocker next to my desk. "I bought you something today—I'll go and get it. Does Nurse Turner know you're down here?"

He sat down, but didn't relax.

"No, she's taking a nap in her chair, and I didn't want to wake her, so I just came down quietly. You bought me something?"

"Hold on, and I'll get it right now. Would you like some tea? I was just going to make myself a cup."

"Thank you, I would love some."

"Good, I also bought some Christmas cookies when I was out today. Would you like some to go with your tea?" I asked, getting up, and starting to head for the kitchen.

Luke got up from the chair, and walked over the look at the computer.

"I would love some, thank you."

He looked down at the keyboard, lost in thought.

"What is it Luke? Do you remember something?"

"Yeah, I was just remembering cookies, and other things I've had, like rolls, and pies. Maybe I live in a bakery."

"That would be nice for you," I laughed.

His gaze went back to the computer screen. "What are you looking at?" he asked.

"That is a satellite view of Canyon Grove. I was just getting a bird's eye view, to see what's there." I pointed out where Main Street was, as well as the school, and train station. "Does any of this look familiar to you, Luke?"

He studied the terrain and shook his head. "I don't remember ever seeing any of it before. I'm sorry."

"That's quite all right, I'm sure if this is where you live, it will come back to you. Right now, what I need to do, is go get your packages, and make our tea."

"Where is Cecilia?" he asked.

She was in the living room looking at a magazine when I last saw her. Why do you ask?"

"I just thought she might want to play some video games with me. She's really good you know."

"No, I didn't know, but then Cecilia is formidable on many fronts. I'm glad you two had fun."

Cecilia entered the room, and saw that Luke was with me.

"There you are, Luke. Nurse Turner was looking for you—she thought you had disappeared, and was frantic. I'll go up and tell her you're with Jillian, so she'll have some peace of mind."

"Ask her if she'd like to join us for some tea. It will be ready in about ten minutes," I said.

"Will do, I'll be back in a second," and off she sailed up the stairs.

Nurse Turner was pleased to be included in our afternoon ritual. I served the tea and Christmas cookies on my best Lenox Holiday china, and placed the tray on the coffee table by the fireplace, next to the beautifully decorated Christmas tree. I gave Luke his new clothes. He was grateful and thanked me, but I don't think he was excited about the popular brands I had bought. It led me to believe that he may have been home schooled, and had no need to keep up with the latest fads his peers were wearing.

After drinking his tea and devouring several cookies, Luke looked expectantly at Cecilia and asked her if she wanted to play some computer games, after we'd had our tea. She gladly complied, and after Nurse Turner told Luke he would have to rest soon, the two of them went to my computer, where Luke played, and Cecilia used her laptop to play on. Nurse Turner and I lingered over another cup of tea, she talking about her family, and I listening, and it felt like Christmas was supposed to feel. I knew it probably wouldn't last, but I decided to enjoy the moment, and was grateful not to be alone. Luke had only been with me for three days, but I had decided that if his parents couldn't be found, I would have no hesitation in adopting him.

❧11❧

Nurse Evans had taken over after dinner, making sure Luke went to bed early, and Walter and Cecilia went for a walk, giving them some time to enjoy being alone together. I made some decaf coffee, to which I added some Hazelnut syrup, and took it to my desk to drink while I finished checking my e-mails.

I suddenly got the urge to check out the Hale AgRecruitment Agency online. The site came up, and looked very official. On the sitemap were the usual topics, such as Home, About Us, and Services. I went through all of them, and was impressed with the number of services available to anyone looking to hire workers. The contact listed was *Grant Hale,* and gave his phone number, and e-mail address.

I scrolled through all of the information, and was ready to exit the site, when I noted a topic on the types of services available. It said, *Special Services,* so I clicked it on. The page was entitled, *Domestic Workers,* and listed various services they could perform, which didn't strike me as being that unusual, until I came to a small footnote in the lower left hand corner. It read, *Finder's Fee Negotiable.*

I was curious as to what that meant, so I decided to Google the term to see if I could find out anything. Finder's Fees referred to realtors, financiers, and horse buyers, but I didn't find anything that related to domestic workers. I would discuss it with Walter, but it looked *irregular* to me.

Teddy followed me upstairs one last time before I retired for the night. I wanted to make sure Nurse Evans had everything she needed, and that Luke was sleeping. Everything seemed fine, so I wished her goodnight and explained that Cecilia would be coming in later, through the front door. I came downstairs again and secured the premises, leaving on a single light for Cecilia to find her way when she came in.

I got ready for bed, taking a lovely relaxing bubble bath as usual, and contemplated all I had learned so far about Luke, Madison, and Quentin Graves.

It made sense that Madison lived close enough to Luke in order to reach him by horseback. Luke must live somewhere isolated if he never had pizza delivered, or had no concept of current fads in clothing. It was also inconceivable that no one had put out a missing persons report on someone as nice as Luke, unless of course someone didn't want any attention brought to them. It would be interesting to talk to the woman who dated Quentin at one time, to see what she knew about him. I was sure he was the same man who was following Madison and Luke. Walter had confirmed that for me, after showing me his picture. Canyon Grove was such a small town that I had to believe someone must know something about Luke, but who? Then, it came to me that a *minister* would know the community and its inhabitants, as well as anyone would.

I had noticed the small church on Main Street, and decided that would be the next thing I would check out in the morning. I sent Ann an e-mail as well, asking her if she was available to go with me in the morning to check out the commune we had seen. I had to find out if it could possibly tie in to Luke.

"Come on Teddy," I said as I gently picked him up, and placed him on his towel at the foot of my bed. I gave him a lot of special pats and strokes, and told him he was coming with me on an outing in the morning.

He flattened his ears against his head, responding to my affection, and communicated that he was ready to get out of the house.

"That's right, you haven't been anywhere with me since the accident, have you?"

He answered with a 'yip' as his answer in the affirmative.

What a smart dog he was.

I prayed that God would continue to help me find the answer to Luke's identity. It was only a half-hearted prayer, though, since I would have been just as happy to adopt him. After all the fresh air I had breathed on my ride, and the warm bath I had just taken, I fell asleep immediately.

Another quiet, uneventful night with Luke passed. In the morning, I felt rested and ready to tackle my special excursion, to meet the inhabitants of the Edwards mansion. I felt in my spirit that I would find answers there.

I checked my e-mails and found one from Ann that said she couldn't come with me today. I was disappointed, but decided I would drive over to Canyon Grove anyway, and see if I could talk to the minister. I also thought that I might find Rick Turner, and see if he knew anything about the commune.

I left a note for Cecilia, since it was still very early, and let Nurse Turner in to take over for Nurse Evans. We exchanged pleasantries, and then Teddy and I were off.

It was a glorious wintry day, even though winter was still officially a few days away. My thoughts turned to Christmas, and I wondered if we would know Luke's identity by then. I didn't even know if I would be placing gifts under the tree for him. It was a bittersweet situation for me. I knew it was probably best to find his parents, but I would miss him if he were to leave.

Since it was still so early by the time I arrived in Canyon Grove, I decided to stop at the Jazz Café for some breakfast. I popped Teddy into his *tres chic* cheetah print carrier, and walked inside.

Iris greeted me from behind the counter, which was filled with lovely looking pastries and donuts.

"Good morning, Jillian, it's nice to see you again. Have a seat anywhere you like."

"Thanks, Iris," I said, taking a seat along the wall close to the door, in case I had to take Teddy out suddenly. She came over to my table, offering me coffee and a menu.

I nodded for her to pour me some coffee.

"I take it black, thanks. I think I'll have a toasted seeded bagel, with cream cheese, and some orange juice, please."

"I'll get it right away."

She went behind the counter, selected a bagel, sliced it in the guillotine, and then popped it in the toaster. I looked around, and saw a couple of patrons having coffee and reading the paper. They looked like they may have been retired and in no hurry to go anywhere. I felt their eyes watching me, wondering why I would have a dog with me. Iris brought me the bagel and juice, and commented on the subject.

"What kind of a dog is that, Jillian?"

"He's a Yorkie. I take him with me whenever I can. He's a very remarkable, little dog, and can understand everything we say."

"Really?" she said, moving away from me, as if I were out of my mind. I finished my breakfast, paid the tab, and reapplied my lipstick.

It didn't take but a minute to drive across the street, and down one block. I parked in the museum parking lot, put Teddy on his leash, and began walking down the sidewalk, to the entrance of the church.

A simple, white sign stood on the small lawn, which read *Church of Canyon Grove*. Dates and times for the services were listed beneath.

Flowerbeds, filled with colorful purple and yellow pansies, adorned the flagstone path leading to the front door. Tall arborvitae and Italian cypress, soaring to the sky, surrounded the white, wooden structure, which must have been at least 100 years old. A bell tower rested on top of the tall steeple. I wondered if the bells rang on Sunday mornings.

Just as I started up the walk, the vicar stepped out from the front door, and was a little startled to see Teddy and me.

"Hello, it's a lovely day, isn't it?" I said.

He looked at Teddy, and me, and smiled.

"It is indeed," he said.

I walked up the path to where he stood.

"I'm Father Perkins."

"And I'm Jillian Bradley. This is Teddy, my companion."

Teddy yipped once, to say "hello."

Father Perkins chuckled, bent down, and offered his hand for Teddy to smell. Teddy wagged his tail in approval, and gave father Perkins an affectionate little lick on his hand. The vicar was delighted. He had been tall as a young man, but now his back was slightly bent. His hands displayed the ravages of arthritis, but his hazel eyes, faded from age, still shone with intelligence, and kindness, as well.

"I'm very happy to meet you, my child. Would you like to come in, and see the church?"

"But weren't you just going out? I don't want to keep you from anything."

"Oh, that's all right. I was just needing to stretch these old legs a bit—it's such a magnificent day that I had to get out in it."

"Well, I'd love to come inside, but I have Teddy with me."

"Oh, that's quite all right—I believe if you hold him that it will be fine. I'm sure he'll let you know if he needs to go outside again."

We both laughed.

"That's fine then. I'd love to see your church."

Father Perkins politely held the door, as Teddy and I entered. After closing the door reverently, he motioned for me to look at the sanctuary.

Morning sunlight streamed in from the East through the four, small, stained glass windows, and spread over the simple wooden pews. A stained glass clerestory window, depicting the cross, stood above the pulpit. A lovely vase of fresh flowers sat on the alter table.

Together, we walked down the aisle, and sat down in the front pew. From the gait of his walk, I judged him to be in his mid-seventies. It struck me that Father Perkins was a man who took the role of shepherding his flock very seriously. Deep lines etched around his eyes had been created by the cares of his parishioners, but when he smiled, those same lines gave him a warm countenance that radiated the love of God. Tall and slightly built, Father Perkins was the epitome of discipline itself. Here was a man who practiced self-control in every area of his life — except for when it came to serving his fellow man.

Teddy rested quietly in my lap, as Father Perkins began to talk.

"Would you like to tell me why you're here in Canyon Grove, Jillian?"

I was truly surprised at his astute perception and straightforwardness, and simply said, "I'm trying to solve a mystery."

He hung his gray head and chuckled, crinkling his feeble eyes that peered out from his wire-rimmed glasses.

"I see. I say, let's resume our conversation outside." He stood and led the way out a back door.

"I have a lovely bench under a lovely tree that rarely gets used, and there's no one to hear, except..." he nodded his head toward the small cemetery, which lay just beyond the back lawn of the church.

Teddy lay down on the soft grass, next to my feet, as the vicar and I sat down on the old wooden bench. I smiled at the beautiful surroundings, and then grew serious.

"I would be very grateful for any information you could give me, regarding a young man we've found who was involved in a car accident, last Saturday afternoon."

He raised his eyebrows in surprise, and said, "Oh my! Who is this young man?"

"That's just the point — he doesn't remember who he is. We think his concussion has given him amnesia. No one has filed a missing persons report, and we've checked the local schools, but there seems to be no record, whatsoever, that we can find."

The vicar was perplexed.

"Well, I'm sure the police have access to fingerprints, and baby footprints on hospital records. Have they tried that?"

"Yes, they took them at the crash site, and nothing showed up."

Father Perkins nodded his head, slowly.

"That is a mystery indeed—almost as if someone doesn't want him to be part of the human race. I'm sorry, I apologize. I don't even know what made me say that. It sounds a bit calloused, don't you think?"

"No, I don't think it sounds calloused. I think we learn more from initial reactions than if we think too hard about something. You have a very good point—what if someone didn't want anyone to know of this boy's existence. Why would that be?"

"Well, let's see now. The first thing that comes to my mind is shame—a child born out of wedlock, perhaps. On the other hand, it could be someone didn't bother to register the birth—which would possibly mean a home birth. You'd be surprised at some of the cases I've seen in my ministry here, although Canyon Grove being a small town—there hasn't been many of that kind. Even if there were, I couldn't divulge any names because of the parishioner's privacy."

"I do understand, and I certainly wouldn't ask you to do anything unethical."

"Thank you, Jillian. However, I'm sure if it meant this boy's salvation, I would be willing to help, perhaps *indirectly*."

"I think I understand, and I appreciate that."

"How old did you say this boy was?"

"According to my doctor, he looks to be about seventeen."

"Seventeen you say."

The vicar was quiet for a moment.

"Is there anything else you know about him?"

"He seems very innocent, as if he's been sheltered somehow. I believe he is home schooled, because in his

112

sleep he's mentioned passing a test. He thinks he has a dog, or had one at one time, and he always thinks fondly of someone baking things for him whenever I serve him cookies. I will tell you, that I've prayed for wisdom to find out who this boy is. My heart goes out to him. Father, he's all alone, and I know he's scared—I can see it in his face."

"Now, now, my child, we'll find out who he is; after all, God knows who he is—we'll just have to trust Him to help us figure it out."

"You've been very kind, Vicar, and I appreciate being able to share this with you. This boy may be in danger of some kind, so we've kept his whereabouts a secret, in case someone means him harm. I'm sure you know about the man who was murdered on Sunday."

"Yes, a man named Quentin Graves. He wasn't one of my parishioners, but I did hear all about it. Someone told me he had a bad reputation over in Clover Hills. It seems he lived a life of debauchery, from what some of my parishioners have told me. It may be hearsay, but usually a man's reputation speaks of his character. I hope you understand what I'm saying, and that I'm only telling you what others have told me. Still, what a horrible way to die."

"The police believe it may be connected to this young man in some way. You can see why I'm so concerned that we find out who he is. He may need our help."

"I do see. Give me your card, Jillian, and I promise I'll help you in any way I can. Please come and see me again, and bring Teddy, won't you?"

"Thank you, Vicar. There's just one more thing."

"Of course, what is it?"

"Do you know how to direct me to Rick Turner's ranch?"

"Rick Turner?"

The vicar looked somewhat taken aback.

"Why, yes, he lives close to here, just about a half-mile up the road. You can't miss it—there's a sign that says, 'Turner Ranch.'"

"Thank you," I said, standing, and starting to leave.

"Is there something about Rick Turner I should know before I go see him? You looked a little concerned when I mentioned his name."

"I'm sorry. I was just wondering why you would want to talk to him. He comes from a fine family who've lived here for years."

"I've heard nice things about him from the Sanders, too. I wanted to see if he knows who lives in the Edwards mansion now."

"You have been busy, haven't you, Jillian? The old Edwards mansion has someone living there? I didn't realize that. No one has seen or heard from anyone there since...."

"Since 1961, when Dorian Edwards disappeared, I know. I'll stop in and see you again soon, I promise. Goodbye, vicar, and thanks for your time."

"Goodbye, my child. Teddy, bring her back to see me."

Teddy yipped that he would indeed.

❧12❧

I found Rick Turner's ranch with no trouble at all. I pulled up in front of the main house, which looked as if it had been constructed entirely of logs, and turned off the ignition. A black and white Border collie raced up to my door and started barking, letting us know that the Turner Ranch was *his* territory. I put the keys in my purse, gathered Teddy in my arms, attached his leash and started to get out of the car.

Rick Turner appeared at the front door, and walked toward us so I waited. He was a little taller than average, and there was not an ounce of fat on his body, probably because he was a hard working rancher. Neatly dressed in a long-sleeved, plaid shirt, jeans, and work boots, (and wearing a Stetson for sun protection), he approached the car and opened the door for me.

"Stay back, Jake," he said, "and let our guests get out of the car."

He tipped his hat as he helped me out, and introduced

himself, extending his rough, calloused hand.

"I'm Rick Turner, and this is my dog Jake."

"Hello, Rick. I'm Jillian Bradley, and this is Teddy, my companion. It's a pleasure to meet you both."

"How can I be of service to you, Jillian?"

"I needed to ask you about some neighbors of yours — the ones who live in the old Edwards mansion."

A lack of comprehension washed over his face, but the look disappeared when he spoke.

"Why don't you come inside, and I'll get you a cup of coffee. I just made a fresh pot."

"That's very kind of you. I would love some."

He held the door open for Teddy and me, as we entered the large, open living room, anchored by a massive stone fireplace. Jake came into the room, and lay down in front of the hearth at Rick's command.

The log walls were decorated with a few nicely framed landscape prints, and the furnishings included deer antler lamps with hide shades, resting on rustic pine side tables, conveniently placed next to comfortable leather couches and easy chairs.

"Your home is very warm, Rick, I don't see how you force yourself to leave it and go to work."

He smiled at the compliment, and I could sense that he was very proud of his house.

"How do you like your coffee?" he asked.

"Black, please. Thanks."

"Can I get Teddy some water? Jake is always thirsty after we've been out."

"Teddy, would you like some water?" I asked.

He pricked up his ears and jumped off my lap, letting me know he did indeed, but I knew he just wanted an excuse to explore Jake's territory.

Rick instinctively understood dogs, I could tell. "I bet

Teddy would like to get acquainted with 'ol Jake here wouldn't he?"

"Come on boys," he called, "into the kitchen, if it's all right with you," he nodded.

"It's fine with me, as long as he can't get into anything — he's very inquisitive."

Rick left to get the coffee, with the dogs following at his heels. A moment later, he walked back into the room and handed me a mug of coffee. I noticed and admired his long tapered fingers — they reminded me of my husband's hands. Funny, I could remember his hands, but had difficulty remembering his face.

"Thanks," I said.

He plopped down in the chair next to the fireplace and spoke.

"So now, tell me about these so called neighbors of mine that you're interested in."

I explained about seeing the house from my ride the other day, and noting the garden. He listened attentively, and seemed genuinely surprised that the house existed at all.

"I'm sorry, but I don't ride beyond my property lines, and that could explain why I've never even seen this place you're talking about. I wish I could be of more help."

"It's quite all right," I said, a little disappointed, "whoever lives there may just be reclusive. I really thought you'd know something, since they live so close."

"From what you've told me, the house would be difficult to see, unless you were viewing it from a certain vantage point, like from the one you did. I suppose that's why I've never seen it. I've lived here all my life, that's the funny thing. My parents live a little ways from here, this used to be part of their property until they deeded it over to me a few years ago. It's taken me awhile to build it up, but I have it to where I want it now."

"What type of ranching do you do?"

"I raise cattle, and I have almond orchards. More coffee, Jillian?"

"Yes, please."

"I'll be back in a minute—I need to check on the boys."

After he left, I walked over to the fireplace, and looked at the various cattle roping trophies displayed on the mantle. He came back into the room, without the coffee, and the look on his face told me something was wrong.

"I'm afraid the dogs have used the dog door to go outside."

"Is that a problem?" I asked, growing a little concerned.

"It is when your dog looks like a meal to a coyote."

He grabbed his shotgun and motioned for me to follow him out the back door.

The dogs were nowhere to be seen. Rick called Jake, and I called Teddy, but there was nothing except silence. Then we heard Jake's bark, and we rushed to where it came from. Rick did not hesitate. Before I even knew what was happening, he fired, and the coyote yelped in pain as the bullet hit him, killing him instantly. I rushed to where Teddy seemed frozen in fear, and yelled his name, "Teddy!"

Rick and Jake walked over to where Teddy sat, shaking.

"He'll be all right, Jillian. He's just in shock from almost being eaten."

I knew that if Rick hadn't shot the coyote when he did, Teddy would have been dead.

"Thank you, Rick, you saved his life!"

"Don't thank me, I should have remembered about that dog door, and never left them alone in the kitchen. Jake can take care of himself, but Teddy is vulnerable because of his size. I apologize for putting you through all this. Let's get him back to the house, so I can fix him up."

I've often wondered why people choose to live alone. While Rick examined Teddy, checking for bite markings, I asked him what he did for entertainment.

He smiled at me, and began picking out the burs from Teddy's coat.

"I play guitar sometimes in front of the fire, or if the weather's good, I sit on the porch, and look at the stars. You can really see them without the lights of the city, except for when the fog rolls in, which is often at this time of year. Sometimes I go over to Clover Hills for dinner, or over to the Jazz Café, and listen to whoever is performing — I lead a quiet life, but it suits me."

Teddy began whimpering, and wanted to jump into my arms, so I petted him gently.

"It's going to be all right, sweet doggie, but you need to be still for Rick."

Teddy looked at Rick, and stood still obediently.

"You're such a *good* dog," I said.

"He is a good dog."

I returned to the conversation with Rick, and asked him if it was difficult to have friends, living as far out as he did. He knew where the conversation was going, and smiled.

"I do have a few friends. I'm a volunteer sheriff's deputy on the weekends, have been for several years. I know you're wondering if I've ever been married, and I'll tell you truthfully that I haven't. As you can see, there aren't too many women to date, when you live as I do."

"I understand, and I didn't mean to pry — it's just my natural tendency to want to see people happily married, even though I know it isn't for everyone."

"I did want to marry someone once. It was a long time ago, but something happened. I think she met someone else, so it didn't work out."

"I'm so sorry. You said you *think* she met someone

else."

Rick averted the question.

"I *think* Teddy should come into the living room, and lie down on the couch. Come on Jake, Jillian, grab our coffee and let's go sit."

Rick gently carried Teddy into the living room, and waited for me to put our coffee down, next to where we had been sitting. He placed Teddy on the couch next to me, and then sat down in his favorite chair. Jake lay down at Rick's feet, and I sipped my coffee, giving him time to tell me his story.

"I guess the long and the short of it is," he began, "I met this girl who worked for the title company we used, when my parents gave me this property. We were both very much in love with each other, or so I thought, and I had asked her to marry me. She said she loved me, but would never give me an answer. Instead of my proposal strengthening our relationship, it seemed to make it grow weaker. Finally, it got to the point where she wouldn't return my calls, so I just assumed she didn't want to marry me, and I quit trying."

"But she never said there was someone else."

"No, she never did, but what else could I think? Like I said, it was a long time ago, and I'm doing fine. I like living alone, it's peaceful, and my cattle and Jake keep me company."

He smiled, and told me about how beautiful it was in the spring, when his almond orchards were in bloom. I began thinking at once about available women I knew, who would make him a good wife.

"I think I'd better be taking Teddy home for some rest and recuperation. Rick, I can't thank you enough for saving his life. That was quick thinking on your part, and I'm very grateful."

"I'm just sorry it had to have happened, but I hope

you'll be careful if you try to find that house — there are coyotes and rattlesnakes all over these hills, and maybe even a cougar or two."

He walked me to my car and opened my door, helping me put Teddy down on the seat next to me, securing him with a rolled up towel. He told me that it was an old one, and didn't need to be returned. He was a good mind reader, I thought, and yet, he wasn't able to read the young woman's mind about their relationship.

❧13❧

I thought I'd better check with Walter, before I decided whether I would venture to find the old Edwards place. I was glad I did. It turned out that the friend of Nurse Turner, who dated Quentin Graves, had moved, and left no forwarding address. I wondered if she had been a victim of his abuse, or had simply moved. Walter also got the report on the car Madison was driving—it was a 1991 Honda Civic CRX sedan. The forensics experts were even able to identify the color—Saxony Blue Metallic. I asked Walter if the owner could be identified, and he assured me they would be able to eventually, but the information had to come from another department and would take a day or two, since it was an older model.

Walter also told me that the microchip found in Luke had been traced to the manufacturer. It would just be a matter of time before they could trace to whom that particular chip was sold. I felt we were on the right track.

I told Walter of the strange term I had noticed, regarding the domestic worker site, and proposed looking into that agency further.

"Jillian, I hope you're not suggesting that you just waltz into the agency, and pretend you're looking for domestic help."

"That's exactly what I'm proposing, Walter. I don't think it would hurt to pay them a call, to satisfy a basic inquiry. After all, I live alone, and I've actually been thinking about changing housekeepers."

"But Jillian, you don't have a housekeeper."

"Exactly, I'll propose to hire one, instead of doing the work myself!"

"I'll go along with it, on one condition. If you will allow me to have you watched from a distance, just to make sure you're safe. Will you agree to that?"

"Not only will I agree—I will feel much safer. Thanks for taking such good care of me, Walter. How soon can you get me a tail?"

"I'll put in a call right now."

Walter lined up the tail for four o'clock. That would give me just enough time to check in on Luke and drop Teddy off.

I stepped inside the house quietly, and closed the kitchen door. Cecilia was in the living room, sitting by the fire, poring over the Bridal magazine once again.

"I think I'm going to suggest to Walter that we have a simple outdoor wedding—it has to cost less than these weddings people have at country clubs. Sorry, Jillian, I was talking to myself aloud again. I was just having a cup of tea—would you like me to make you a cup?"

"I suppose I have a little time, thank you, Cecilia. "You know, you and Walter are welcome to use my house if you want. There's a perfect place for the ceremony in the gazebo."

"Really? But wouldn't that be an imposition for you?"

"Not if *you* planned the whole thing, in fact, I think it would be fun. Talk to Walter, and see what he thinks."

"I will. Thank you!"

"Frankly, I think your frugality is one of your attributes, and Walter is going to be fortunate having you for his wife. How is Luke, by the way? Is he awake?"

Cecilia rose to make the tea.

"He just went down for a nap after Nurse Turner gave him his sedative. We've had quite a morning playing video games. He's very adept at the computer. And, I have to tell you, he's had another recall."

"Really, what did he say?"

I followed Cecilia into the kitchen and sat at the table, as she prepared my tea.

"Well, he became a little transfixed, and said he remembered wild turkeys, soaring hawks overhead, and coyotes howling in the distance. And he said that he remembered being alone, outside, but wasn't afraid. I thought it all sounded very strange, coming from a teenager."

Cecilia set the cup of tea before me, and sat down.

"I would have to agree, unless he lived on a farm somewhere, and there are a few, I'm sure, around Canyon Grove."

I drank my tea, and looked at my watch. It was almost time to visit the agency.

I confided my plans to Cecilia, which caused her to become distressed, but after I told her I would have someone watching me, she acquiesced, and thought it was probably the only way to find out what was really going on there.

"Good luck!" she wished me, as I headed out the door.

Off I went, posturing myself as a wealthy widow, in search of domestic help that I could possibly bully. I would soon know what type of people ran this business, just by their reactions to my type of inquiry!

The man at the front desk seemed a little surprised to see me. He wore a suit, but had removed his jacket, and rolled up his sleeves to work at his computer more comfortably. He told me that he would be with me in a minute, and put on his suit coat, and then straightened his tie. I glanced around the office, with a snobbish air, and waited for him to finish dressing. There were two assistants sitting at desks, busy at their computers. Each glanced up briefly when I entered, but returned to their work as soon as the man in the suit stood up to wait on me.

"Now then," he said with a smile, "how can I help you?"

"I'm looking for some domestic help, and came across your website. I've noticed your agency before, and decided to come in and have a chat."

The man seemed unsure of how to proceed, and so I decided to be forthright.

"I'm simply tired of keeping up with my house and feel it's time to hire someone, preferably someone who can live in, and do the chores. Do you have these types of workers available?"

"Why don't we step into my private office where I think we'll be more comfortable," the man replied, with a smile of assurance that indeed they did.

"I'm sure we can find exactly what you need. My name is Grant Hale by the way, and you are?"

"My name is Jillian Bradley. I'm a gardening columnist for *The San Francisco Enterprise*. I'm sure you're heard of me," I said, proudly.

"Oh, the name *does* sound familiar. I'm sure we have just what you're looking for, Mrs. Bradley."

"That's fine, now what I had in mind was someone young, you know, able to do a lot of work without too many breaks, and someone not so educated that they'll want to move on after a month or two, you know the type. I want someone who will stay on for a *long* time, that is, if I'm going to invest my time *training* them."

"Oh, yes, I can see that you know exactly what you want, and I think we can find a match." Mr. Hale began searching his computer base, as I fumbled in my purse for my checkbook.

"Here we are," he said, "I think I have just the young woman you're looking for."

"How soon can she begin?" I asked, not even looking at the computer.

"It takes a few days to notify her of the position opening, but I would think we could have her installed within the week."

"That's splendid, how much?" I asked without any appearance of concern over price.

Mr. Hale looked rather pleased at my apparent acceptance and lack of specific questions, and proceeded to explain the financial options.

"We deal with domestics of all types and situations, you understand, and it is entirely up to you of course, but we have domestics who are paid wages on a monthly basis, and then we have a few who are willing to work for room and board. The latter are not as fluent in English as the former...."

"Let's not beat about the bush, Mr. Hale. I don't care where they come from, how they get here, or if they can speak English, or not. I'm sure I can make them understand what I want."

"Well then, you may want to invest in someone who will work for room and board."

"If it will save me money in the end, yes. I was also wondering about something I read on your site that said, a finder's fee was negotiable. Is that what you're talking about here?"

"As a matter of fact, it's a term we use when discussing the fee we charge for finding a domestic, such as one I was telling you about."

"I see, so what is your finder's fee for what I want?"

Mr. Hale raised his eyebrows, and said simply, "$1,500."

"And for $1,500, I get a maid, who will come live with me, and do my bidding, is that correct?"

"That is correct, Mrs. Bradley. Do you wish for me to proceed?"

"That's quite a bargain! But I suppose there are struggling individuals, willing to work for food and shelter. Can you guarantee they're not criminals?"

"We do a thorough background check, yes."

"What if they want to leave after I've paid for them?"

"I'm only able to tell you that we have certain security precautions put in place that keep them from leaving. We make them understand that they are *very* fortunate to get these positions, and we have very little trouble, I can assure you. We even offer a money back guarantee if you're not completely satisfied, after a certain length of time. I'm sure you'll agree our service is most equitable."

I acted as if I was satisfied with the arrangement.

"Will you take a check?"

"Unfortunately, we only deal in cash. It's so much simpler because of all the government regulations, nowadays. It's quite acceptable — you'd be surprised at how many people acquire help this way these days."

"Yes, I've even heard of government people with illegal aliens as housekeepers. I'll wait to hear from you as soon as you can bring my maid to me, and I'll have your cash ready. I'll look forward to next week then," I said, handing him my card. I closed my purse, and turned to leave.

"I'll call you when the arrangements have been made, Mrs. Bradley, thank you for stopping in. It was a *pleasure* meeting you."

"I'll look forward to hearing from you, Mr. Hale." I strode confidently out of the office, and got into my car, my hand shaking as I turned on the ignition.

I pulled out of the parking space slowly, and tried not to glance around to see my tail. No one followed me home, I was sure, and I didn't see anyone who even remotely looked like an undercover officer.

Did I get away with it? Grant Hale seemed quite pleased to make such a simple transaction. No paperwork, no trail of any kind to incriminate him of any criminal offense. How many others had made a deal like mine, I wondered. I would wait until I returned home before calling Walter. Hopefully, he would now be able to check up on Mr. Grant Hale.

❧14❦

I noticed the plain-clothes officer parked down the street, and was grateful he looked up when I pulled into my driveway. Teddy yipped constantly when I came in the door—he was so excited to see me. I picked him up, and lavished hugs and kisses on top of his sweet little brown head.

"What have you been up to today? Have you kept Luke company?" I set him on the floor, and he followed me into the hallway as I took off my coat and hung it up on the coat rack, along with my purse. I had seen Walter's car parked in front of the house, and knew he was here to see Cecilia. That was convenient for me—I had so much to tell him.

Cecilia greeted me from the living room, and asked how my afternoon went. Luke was on the floor playing tug of war with Teddy and one of his stuffed toys. Oh, how Teddy loved to play that game. He was growling fiercely, just like a big dog, trying to wrestle the stuffed rabbit away from Luke, and Luke was smiling, growling back, having such a good time. I was glad he was feeling better. I knew everyone would be hungry, so I announced I would be in the kitchen if anyone wanted to talk to me. Immediately, all four (including Teddy) followed me into the kitchen.

"I'm just going to make Rachel Ray's Vegetable Soup tonight—it's quick and easy, and we all need more vegetables." I donned my apron, and began getting out all the ingredients.

"Can we help?" Luke asked.

"You certainly may."

Cecilia and Walter pitched in as well, and before long, the hearty soup boiled to perfection. We called for Nurse Turner to join us, and all sat down and enjoyed our meal together. Luke reiterated what he had recalled, about the hawks flying overhead, and seeing the wild turkeys and coyotes. I told him I thought he had to live in Canyon Grove, if those were part of his memory. He excused himself to go play with Teddy some more in the living room. Nurse Turner followed him.

I was glad to have the opportunity to talk to Walter without Luke present. I still had no idea how such a nice young man could be connected to illegal immigration.

"Well, Jillian," Walter began, "you've either hired yourself a housekeeper, or stirred up someone's illegal operation of importing domestic labor."

"I think you're right; either way, we'll see soon enough. How are you coming along with the microchip information?"

"I just received information that confirms Luke's microchip was sold to a local vet, here in Clover Hills. I'm going to pay him a visit in the morning. His story should prove interesting."

"I plan to check out that garden I saw the other day

with Ann. I'll take Teddy along for protection. I'm hoping to find someone there who may know where Luke lives."

"Ann's going with you, isn't she?" asked Cecilia. "I don't think you should go alone."

"She said she would, but she can be awfully busy during the holidays. I'm sure I'll be fine. I'll have my cell phone with me, and Teddy is a good judge of character, in case I'm not. I'll send her an e-mail and see if she'd like to come."

Luke came into the kitchen, looking dazed. Cecilia, Walter, and I looked at him, and asked what the matter was.

"I just remembered something else."

"Tell us, Luke, what did you remember?"

"I saw myself, and a girl, riding horses—we were out in the country, and we were the only ones around. I could see her smiling at me, and we were having a good time together. She had blond hair...I remember her name now, it was...Madison." Luke stumbled forward, feeling faint, and Walter caught him in his arms.

"I think we better get him upstairs to bed," I said, "He's had a shock." Nurse Turner helped him into bed, and got his sedative ready. I called Dr. Peters, and told him what Luke had said.

"He sounds like he's getting closer to the present time, Jillian. I think you should stay with him until he remembers who he is. It could be traumatic."

"I understand, Dr. Peters. If I'm away, Cecilia and a nurse will be here, and I can always be reached by cell phone."

"I'll be anxious to hear of any more developments, so please call me."

"Thank you, Dr. Peters, we will. Goodbye."

I returned to Luke's room and pulled a chair up close to his bed.

"How are you feeling?" I asked, softly.

"I'm a little tired—I feel drained. At least I remembered something—that's good, isn't it?"

"Luke, I need to tell you something, but before I do, you need to know that I truly believe you're going to come out of this all right. You're young, and well brought up, and you have people here who care about your welfare. I think somewhere, there must be others who care about you, too."

"Then why haven't they found me?"

"I can't answer that. I only know that I'm praying God will help us get you home. Do you pray, Luke?"

"I can't remember if I do or not."

"Praying is talking to God. He hears us, and will answer with either a yes, no, or not yet. I think the answer is not yet, but I continue to pray for answers. We're still looking for clues, and Walter is working as hard as he can to help us."

Luke shook his head in understanding, and then looked me in the eye, with a look of dread on his face. "What do you want to tell me, Jillian?"

"This is very hard for me to tell you, but I think you need to know. The girl you remembered as Madison was the one who was driving the car when you crashed."

"Then she'll know who I am!"

"She would have…."

"She's dead, isn't she?"

"I'm afraid so. I'm so sorry, Luke."

"I'm sorry, too. I can't remember a whole lot about her, but I believe she was my friend."

"Luke, we know that there were men following her car before it crashed, do you remember that?"

Luke turned his head to the wall, and considered what I'd said.

"I can't remember anything about the crash at all. I only

remember Teddy being with me, and then you brought me here. I'm sorry."

"It's okay, but when you do remember, perhaps we'll learn why you and Madison were running away. Now you get some sleep, I'll have Nurse Turner give you your sedative now. Sleep well, and I'll see you in the morning."

"Goodnight, Jillian, and please keep praying for me."

"I certainly will, I promise."

The lights were turned down low in the living room, and I knew that Walter and Cecilia probably wanted to be alone. Still, after I descended the stairs, Cecilia came to me, and said she would be happy to lock up so I could get to bed. I thanked her, and after making sure Teddy had been taken outside, retired to my bedroom for the night. It had been quite a day—Luke's recollections, which I counted as a good thing for him—my visit to Hale's recruitment agency, and Luke's understanding that he had not only the support of his new friends, but the support of prayer, which can be powerful.

I turned off the lights and crawled into bed, a little weary, but anxious to visit the mysterious estate tomorrow morning. I saw the weather report, and knew a rainstorm was coming in from the North, but it wasn't supposed to reach our area until tomorrow evening. Ann had affirmed her plans to join me at the Jazz Café tomorrow, even though she felt a little tired, so at least that was in place. Now, for a good night's sleep.

It was not to be. Teddy began growling again, and started barking furiously at 2 a.m. I got out of bed to look out the window. I had enough presence of mind not to turn on the light, and had plenty of moonlight to see what was causing him to bark. I looked out onto my backyard and searched, from one end to the other. Nothing moved. Maybe it was a false alarm. I would have to check in the morning to see if anything was amiss. Teddy calmed down, and we both tried going back to sleep. But I started to think about the fact that I had given my card to Grant Hale — that meant he had my address and phone number. Maybe he was checking *me* out. It was difficult getting back to sleep, but I knew I had to be rested for my excursion the next day, so I forced myself to stop thinking, and finally fell back asleep. Before I knew it, the clock said 7:00 a.m. Nurse Evans waved goodbye, as Nurse Turner reported for duty, all ready to go to work. I wished I felt the same. I put on my robe and took Teddy through the conservatory, so he could go outside, and was shaken to find the back door ajar. The lock had been jimmied!

"It looks like you were right, Teddy; someone tried to get in last night. I think you probably scared them off!" I called Walter immediately.

He picked up on the first ring and sounded very upset that someone got past his man.

"I'll have the officer in front of your house check it out — I can't believe he didn't see them!"

"Whoever it was must have realized there was a stakeout, and sneaked in the back. Walter, I'm pretty shaken. If Teddy hadn't barked, we might have had an intruder."

"I'm calling right now, Jillian. Now don't worry, we've got you covered. I'll post a man in back as soon as possible — I'm sorry you had a scare like that."

"I'll be all right. Make your call, and let me know how soon he can start watching the back."

The officer watching the front soon knocked at the door, and together we searched the back yard for evidence. The back door looked like someone had taken a crowbar to it, forcing the lock. I suddenly grew fearful that someone might be trying to get Luke back. I would get Cecilia to have the door repaired as soon as possible. I didn't want Luke to know — it would only upset him to know someone might be trying to kidnap him. No, I was going to find out all I could about that house, before anything else happened.

I got dressed as quickly as I could, made myself a bagel with cream cheese, and put my coffee in a paper go cup. With Teddy in tow, ears cocked up and ready for action, I headed for Canyon Grove where I was to meet Ann.

There were a few cars parked in front of the Jazz Café when I arrived, but I didn't see Ann's anywhere. She usually arrived way before I did. My phone rang, and sure enough, it was her.

"Jillian, I'm so sorry, but I've come down with the flu and I'm going to have to stay in bed. Will you be all right?"

"I'm sorry you're sick, Ann, but I think I'll be all right, I have Teddy with me. You get some rest, and I hope you feel better soon."

I suddenly realized I was on my own.

"Lord, please go with me and protect me," I prayed.

Clouds began to form overhead, and I remembered that rain was forecast. The storm was not due for a few hours, so I still had time for my interview. I felt a little queasiness in my stomach, but my determination to uncover the mystery of that house soon dispelled the feeling.

The road beside the rock markings (that I had discovered earlier) led to the house, as I had thought. The strange part, however, was that the road ended at the *back* of the house where the garden was, instead of the front. I figured it was probably easier to park their cars in the detached garage, behind the garden.

I noted what looked like an old carriage house, badly in need of paint, a few yards from the garage.

A man, dressed in overalls, was tending the garden as I

drove up. I waved a friendly hello, parked the car, and stepped out the door, holding Teddy in my arms, with his leash attached, just in case.

The man stopped hoeing, and just looked at me without any expression on his square, ruddy face. His nose was too large for his face, and his ears were smaller than normal.

"Hello there," I began. "I hope you don't mind my paying you a visit, but I saw your garden the other day when I was out for a ride, and wanted to take a better look at it."

I held out my hand, and introduced Teddy and myself. At the mention of his garden, the man's eyes came alive. I could see immediately that this was his life, and it was a beautiful one.

There were no fallow rows—every one of them was bursting with vegetables. I noted the rows had been planted according to their kind. Rows of leafy vegetables included: chard, spinach, kale, mustard, endive, and lettuce—both red leafed, and romaine. There were rows of root vegetables, containing beets, carrots, radishes, onions, leeks, garlic, parsnips, fennel, and kohlrabi. Rows of flowering vegetables, broccoli and cauliflower, were next to the pod vegetables of English peas, sugar peas, and broad beans. I also noted a row dedicated to the Asian vegetables—bok choy and snow peas. The final row contained two European varieties of arugula and dandelion, along with at least six different herbs growing next to them.

The gentle giant reached for Teddy, wanting to hold him—Teddy went to him without hesitation, which I took as a good sign that this was a friend. The man took Teddy very carefully, supporting his legs, and tummy.

"I like him," he said, haltingly.

"I like him, too," I replied.

He gave Teddy a small kiss on top of his head, just as I

do all the time. I was touched. The man pointed to the Coastal Gem Grevilleas he had planted as a border. The red blooms stood out magnificently against the gray-green foliage.

"These for humming birds," he informed me, proudly.

Suddenly, the man smiled and whistled, calling someone. A huge, tan and black Mastiff appeared, wagging his long tail and barking, letting us know he was ready to protect his property.

I had never seen such a large dog in all my life! He stood as tall as my shoulders, and must have weighed several hundred pounds. The man set Teddy down in front of the giant tan dog with the black face and paws. Please don't eat him, I thought.

The huge beast didn't quite know what to do with the tasty morsel set before him. He looked at his master, and then back at Teddy. My fearless dog started to yip at the giant creature, as if to say, "Well, say, 'hello' you big dumb dog!"

The Mastiff let out a low, gruff bark, as if to reply, "What are you supposed to be, a dog?"

"His name...Ambrose," the man stuttered. "He like Teddy...he like you."

"Well, he's a wonderful guard dog, I can see that. Is this your garden?" I asked, pointing to the amazing winter crop.

The man nodded proudly.

The dogs started the ritual of becoming acquainted by sniffing each other, and then falling into a huge romp after each decided the other wasn't a threat. Please don't roll over on him, I thought.

"What is your name?" I asked.

"My name...Virgil. I live here."

After a slight pause, he said, "Wait here."

The sky grew darker in preparation for the rain to

descend.

He went back into the house, while Ambrose remained with us still wagging his long tail. A few moments later, Virgil reappeared with an elderly woman coming out in front of him, drying off her hands with a dishtowel, apparently to check us out. Virgil carried a bowl of fresh water for Teddy, and set it down next to the house.

"Can I help you?" she asked, politely. "If you're lost, I can direct you back to the main road."

"No, we're not lost at all. I'm Jillian Bradley, and this is my dog, Teddy. We saw your garden when we were out for a ride the other day, and since I'm a gardening columnist, I had to have a closer look, that's all. Do you mind if I find out how you keep such a beautiful winter crop going at this time of year? It's really amazing!" I said, hoping the flattery would make them comfortable with me.

"I suppose you could ask Virgil here, he's a bit slow, but he sure knows how to garden. He keeps us in vegetables and flowers the whole year round. He's my son. The name's Kate Edwards."

I had found them.

Kate wore a spattered apron over a simple homemade dress, and looked more like an old cook than a matriarch. Her short gray hair looked as if she trimmed it herself. Her face was square, like Virgil's, but there was intelligence in her eyes that I didn't find in Virgil's'. She seemed like someone who had been cut off from the modern world.

I immediately said how nice it was to meet her, and even though she didn't accept my hand to shake, after I handed her my card, she seemed to believe my reason for being there.

"Would you like to come in? Looks like it's going to rain any minute. The dogs can stay outside and run around for a while. Ambrose will look after your 'puff ball' there, so he'll be all right."

After my experience with the coyote at Rick Turner's ranch, I was hesitant, but at this point, I had to trust Ambrose to look after Teddy.

"Why, thank you, it's very kind of you to give me an interview."

Virgil remained outside for a few minutes to finish weeding a particular row of red lettuce, and then joined us in the kitchen as it began to rain.

I took out a notebook that I had brought for the occasion, and began asking all sorts of questions regarding soil, fertilizers, amendments, seeds, and anything else I thought would make an interesting article for my column.

"I think that will do nicely," I said, putting the notebook back into my purse. "Would you mind letting my dog back inside? He's afraid of thunder."

"Virgil, get her dog inside."

Virgil dutifully obeyed.

Kate rose, and asked if I would like a cup of tea. I assured her I would love one, if it was no trouble, and she motioned for me to follow her into the living room. She motioned to the couch.

"Have a seat," she nodded. "I'll go get the tea ready."

"Thank you," I said, taking a seat on the faded divan.

The room was filled with old Victorian furniture—a wealth of antiques. A kerosene heater burned in the fireplace, and I wondered if the house had electric heating. Virgil brought Teddy to me and then he returned to the kitchen to watch the rain falling on his garden.

"Nora?" Kate called, rather loudly.

A haggard-looking young woman wearing a well-worn apron appeared quickly and waited for Kate's order.

I couldn't tell what was wrong with her, but there was something not quite right. There were dark circles under her eyes where there should not have been at her age, and her shoulders were slumped, as if she did physical labor all day long.

"Yes, ma'am?' she said, softly, with a definite air of servitude.

"Bring us the tea, and some of those cookies I just baked this morning, and be quick about it!" she added, unkindly. "You'll have to excuse Nora, she's shy around strangers."

I nodded a polite acknowledgement, and glanced around the room. The carpets and drapes were threadbare, and very few accessories graced the tables. Old landscape prints hung here and there on the walls, and I believed everything must have been original to the house. There were no photographs displayed anywhere that I could see, either on the mantle, or on any of the tabletops. The most curious observation I made, however, was that there were no Christmas decorations anywhere, not even a small tree. Then again, it could have been due to a religious conviction of some type, but I had a feeling that wasn't the case.

I heard a car drive up, and someone opening and closing the car door. Were there more visitors to this remote property? Someone came in through the front door, but I couldn't see who it was since my back was facing it. Kate nodded a look of recognition, and turned to look at me.

"You must meet my son, Phillip. I'll have Nora tell him you're here when she brings the tea."

"Why, thank you, I'd love to meet him. So, both of your sons live with you, here?" I asked, conversationally.

"They've lived with me all their life."

Nora brought in a large tray, filled with a pot of tea and a plate of delicious looking cookies, and served us very formally.

"Nora, after you've finished, go tell Phillip we have a guest that I'd like for him to meet. Tell him I expect him to come at once."

"Yes, ma'am," Nora said obediently, as she finished pouring our tea, and offering us cookies. "I'll tell him right away."

There were questions I wanted to ask. However, something cautioned me not to mention Luke. I turned around to look when I heard Nora leading Phillip into the room. She waited in the doorway until she was dismissed. For a brief moment, I saw her look at Phillip with a look of contempt, but then she assumed the impassive posture of a servant.

Kate seemed to ignore her temporarily, and beamed when she saw Phillip.

"That will be all for now, Nora," Kate said.

Nora quietly withdrew into the hall.

"Come in Phillip," Kate beckoned, lovingly. "We have a guest with us."

Phillip sauntered into the room.

"This is Jillian Bradley, a gardening columnist with *The San Francisco Enterprise,* who's come to learn about our garden."

"It's a pleasure to meet you, Jillian. I'm Phillip Edwards."

I knew from Hope's report on the Edwards family, that he was in his late fifties, but I wasn't prepared for how sophisticated he was, or how confidently he carried himself. Slender and fit, with dark hair and eyes, Phillip Edwards could only be described as handsome. Whereas Virgil favored Kate, Phillip was Virgil's opposite in every way, perhaps taking after his father. Virgil was simple—a man who worked with his hands. Phillip was charming—a man who worked with his mind. He sat down, but declined tea, when Kate offered to get another cup.

"I apologize, Jillian, but I have a lot of work to do."

"What kind of work do you do, Mr. Edwards?" I asked, taking the last sip of my tea.

"I'm in business acquisitions — sales — commodities, that sort of thing. I have the luxury of running it from my home, which allows me to work in peace and quiet instead of a noisy office."

"I know what you mean, I work at home, too," I replied, trying to replace my cup on the saucer. I felt a little nauseous, but rationalized that it must be my nerves.

"Are you feeling all right, Jillian?" Phillip asked. "Would you like to lie down?"

"No, I'm fine, thank you. Tell me, and please don't think I'm rude, but I think I read once about the history of the Edwards family — I believe it was when I visited the museum in Canyon Grove the other day, prior to my ride. Are you descendants of this same family?"

Kate looked at Phillip with unhappiness in her eyes, "Will you please excuse me, Jillian? I think I'll check on Virgil and the dogs."

"Why of course."

"I suppose it's no secret that we're descendants of Uriah and Rebecca Edwards. I would imagine you've heard the story of my father who disappeared years ago."

"I'm so sorry. There was never any clue to where he may have gone?"

"Sad to say, no. I was only seven when he went away."

The nausea began to return, but I willed it not to show. I hoped I wasn't getting the flu, like Ann.

"What was he like? Can you remember him at all?" I asked.

"I remember that I loved him. And he was a good father — I also remember that. I have a few memories of him taking us hunting and fishing. Sometimes he'd let us go to the olive groves with him, and he would teach us about how they grew."

Phillip had a fond, faraway look in his eyes as he spoke.

"He sounds like a wonderful father."

"The last thing I remember was his playing with me one day, and then my mother telling me that he wasn't well, and said he couldn't play with me for a while. I was sad for a time, and then soon after that, Mother said our father had gone away."

"Did she say where he went?"

"No, whenever I asked her about him, she refused to say anything at all, so I quit asking. Virgil and I assumed he must have found another woman, or something like that must have happened. It was really so long ago."

Kate reappeared with Teddy in her arms. He was struggling to get free, but Kate held him tight.

"I brushed him off for you. He really got dirty playing with Ambrose out there. You may have to give him a bath...."

My mind went blank as Kate's voice faded in the background. I leaned over on my right side, and everything went black.

❧15❧

As I slowly regained consciousness, my first instinct was to reach in my right pants pocket, take out my cell phone, and call Walter for help. The phone was gone. The nausea, however, was not. My throat was parched, as if I hadn't had anything to drink for several hours. I pried one eye open, and then the other, but found myself in utter darkness.

A dim outline of a window began to form, as my eyes grew accustomed to the darkness. I must be in a bedroom somewhere, I thought. My head was swimming, with faint memories of Teddy being handed to me by Kate, her smiling at me in feigned innocence, and then passing out.

Gradually, I managed to put both feet on the ground and sat up for a moment, to get my bearings. I stood up slowly and went to the window, only to discover that it had been nailed shut and covered with blackout drapes. I shuffled to the door, steadying myself as best as I could. I tried turning the handle, but it had been locked from the outside. Pressing my ear to the door, I tried listening for any sound of life, hoping I would hear my precious Teddy somewhere, barking for me.

There was only silence.

I banged on the door and called for someone to help me, as politely as I could, still giving my hosts the benefit of the doubt. Then I remembered that someone had taken my cell phone, and I knew immediately that I had fallen right into the middle of something very sinister.

The nausea subsided, unlike flu symptoms, and I deduced that one of them had put something in my tea to cause me to pass out. I wouldn't fall *prey* to that again!

I continued listening at the door until I heard light footsteps approach. I staggered back to the bed and lay back down, but I would let whoever came in know that I was awake.

A key turned slowly in the lock, and someone opened the door slightly to check on me.

"Are you awake, Mrs. Bradley?" the quiet voice inquired.

I wasn't sure if I could even answer because my throat was so parched, but I was able to say, "Yes."

Nora stepped into the room and locked the door behind her. She set a small tray down on a table near the door, and turned on a small light, sitting on top of a dresser.

"I brought you some water, and something to eat."

"That was kind of you, Nora."

She placed the tray on my lap and stepped back, fearful I suppose that I might try to escape, and started to leave the room.

"How long have I been here?"

"I'm not supposed to talk to you."

"Well, can you tell me if my dog is all right?"

"He's all right. Now, please, drink your *water* and eat

your supper. I have to go."

Nora left the room quickly, locking the door after she left.

"At least Teddy is all right, thank you, Lord!" I whispered.

I stared at the water, and decided not to drink it. The food looked okay, but I couldn't be sure it wasn't drugged. I'll make them think I drank the water, but there's no way I'm going to eat anything, I said to myself.

I poured out the water slowly onto the carpet under the bed, where it wouldn't draw attention. I stirred the food a little, to look as if I'd eaten some of it. I had no choice but to wait until someone came to check on me. I might as well sleep while I can, I thought. As I lay back down on the bed, I could hear a storm approach, and then I remembered one was due in the evening. That meant that I had only been here a few hours!

It rained all night long, without letting up. No one came to my room during the night, even though I heard doors opening and closing, with hushed voices carrying on conversations. There was only a bedpan to use for a toilet, but it had a cover, at least. This house was truly antiquated! I wondered why nothing had been done to modernize it, unless of course only *some* of the rooms had been, like Phillip's office, perhaps.

I had parted the drapes, just slightly, so I would be able to tell when it was daylight. When I awoke the next morning, I went to the window, and glanced carefully out, onto the back of the house. Kate was in the flooded garden talking to Virgil, pointing up to my room. I didn't think they were able to see me—I prayed they didn't.

They probably thought I was still drugged, so I lay back down on the bed, thinking Virgil may be on his way to check on me.

I heard a train whistle three times in the distance. Was it a signal for a cargo being delivered?

After a few minutes there was a commotion outside the door, and someone (it sounded like Kate) said:

"We'll decide what to do with her later, right now, you have business to attend to, so get to it!"

I heard the door being unlocked, so I feigned sleep. I think it must have been Kate. I didn't hear anyone else approach, or leave after she gave her last order. I held my breath as she looked in on me.

"Better get Nora up here to get rid of the filth," she said, under her breath. "Sleep well while you can, you fool," she muttered, closing the door, and locking it behind her.

It would take a miracle for me to get out of this.

"Lord," I prayed, "I trust You to help me. Show me what to do."

Someone *had* to be looking for me after I didn't return home yesterday afternoon! Surely, they would try to reach Ann, and she could tell them how to get here, unless the rain last night made the road too muddy to drive on. Even if they reached the house, they would need a search warrant, and I knew that took at least a day to get ready. I was just going to have to find a way to escape. I saw no other way around it.

At last, I heard the key turn in the lock, with Nora entering the room with another tray of food and water. She locked the door carefully behind her, and set the tray down, as before.

I decided I had to take a chance. I sat up slowly, trying not to alarm her.

"You don't seem to be a willing part of all this, won't you please help me?" I pleaded.

Nora hesitated at first, but then she seemed to make up her mind.

"I'll help you, but they must never find out or I'm afraid they'll kill me!"

"I understand," I said, as she placed a key in my hand.

Nora left quickly, taking the pot and tray away and locking the door behind her.

I put the key in my pocket, and lay down on the bed, feigning unconsciousness, once again, until the coast was clear. It wasn't long until I heard heavy footsteps coming up the stairs toward my room. The doorknob turned without a key. Nora must have left it open! No one came in, but I heard the door being locked, again. The person just walked away, as if they'd changed their mind. The next thing I heard was heavy knocking on the door next to my room, and Kate began to yell!

"Nora, open this door immediately!"

I heard a door open, and then close again.

I was terrified! I had to remind myself that I must keep my wits about me, or I would never get out of this mess. I got up and listened through the wall, to hear what Kate was saying. She was angry enough to kill someone. I prayed for the Lord to protect Nora.

Kate started yelling again: "You've made a fatal mistake in trying to help that woman escape! I know you took that extra key! Only you would betray me like that!"

I could hear Nora beginning to cry, but there was nothing I could do to help her. Kate continued her rampage:

"Is this how you repay me for taking you in — for feeding you all these years — for giving you a roof over your head, and sheltering you from the world? Is this how you thank me for all I've done for you, Nora? You're nothing but a slut really, a pathetic, whiney slut."

I could hear Nora crying loudly, as if she wanted to die.

Kate started in on her again, loudly at first, and then she spoke in quieter tones, so I was unable to understand what she was saying. Kate's voice suddenly rose again:

"Go ahead — cry, and whine all you want — there's no one to hear you. You'll be out of your misery very soon now — I'll see to that. And don't worry, I'll make sure you die quickly, I've had plenty of practice you know. Oh, yes, I've had plenty of practice."

So Kate confessed to being a murderer!

Nora had stopped crying, and I could hear Kate locking the door as she left the room.

I felt fear rising in my throat.

Kate wasted no time. She unlocked my door, and sauntered in the room, as if she was a spider headed for its prey.

I lay still on the bed, hoping I could fool her to think that I was unconscious.

She walked over to my bed, pulled up a chair, and stuck a gun to my forehead.

"You can stop pretending now. I know Nora was helping you escape."

I opened my eyes slowly, and forced myself not to show fear. I sat up, with her still pointing the gun at my forehead. The look in her eyes made me believe she wouldn't hesitate to pull the trigger.

"Sit up slowly," she commanded.

I did as I was told.

"Let's have the key, Jillian."

I reached into my pocket, and handed her the key. She held me with her cruel eyes, as she took it from me.

"Nora was a fool to have tried to help you. She'll pay for that with her life. I'm afraid I'll have to kill you, too — you really should have minded your own business."

I thought of a retort, but I decided not to say anything — Kate was obviously so insane, that I knew nothing I said would deter her from carrying out her threat against me. I would let her indicate her next move. I thought she would be taking me somewhere to shoot me. I wasn't prepared for what she told me.

Kate waved the gun as she spoke, and decided I wasn't a flight risk. She still held the gun with one finger on the trigger, but rested it in her lap, for the moment.

She had my full attention.

"Shall I tell you about the people I've put out of their misery before you join them? I think I'd enjoy telling someone. I've kept it to myself for so long, for so very long."

I simply nodded, grateful for the reprieve.

"Shall I begin with Dorian? He was the first. You see, my father was dirt poor, and he owed Dorian a great deal of money, so he made a deal with him. Dorian's wife Elsa had died suddenly, and he was very lonely. My father offered me as payment for his debt. I was only sixteen.

"I wanted to get away from my miserable existence so badly—I did all the hard work around the house. I cooked for my father, and helped with the feed business he had. So I agreed to marry Dorian, to better myself.

"He was much older than I was, and of course, we had nothing in common. He was never satisfied with me, except in bed. Back then, I was really pretty, people said. I was so young—he took me over and over, every night, until I was pregnant. I think that's all he wanted—children to carry on his name, and his inheritance.

"Phillip was born ten months after we were married. I barely recovered, when I got pregnant again with Virgil.

"I began to really *hate* Dorian. I meant nothing to him, not really. He was still in love with Elsa—he even called me her name when he took me.

"Eventually, I was nothing more than an object for his lust. That's all I was to him, a thing, a convenience. I started hating him with a vengeance, and then one day I figured out

I had to get away from him somehow. I couldn't stand for him to touch me, and I began to look for a way out.

"It came one afternoon as Dorian was coming from the carriage house, with a sack of arsenic in his hand. He told me he was ridding the garage of vermin. That's what he said — 'Getting rid of vermin.' He said it so matter of fact, and I thought to myself, that's what I should do, get rid of the vermin.

"Dorian had gone into town to buy some feed, and I found the bag of arsenic. I removed about a cup, and took it to the house. I remember putting it into a tin, and marking it, castor oil powder, so the boys would never touch it.

"I began putting pinches into Dorian's breakfast. He always ate oatmeal — he loved it. He was so simple! Little by little he grew weak, and I would take over more and more of his paperwork, 'to help him out.'

"Toward the end, he told me all about his business, the way he got workers illegally, and what happened to some of them. He sensed he was seriously ill, and told me, if anything should happen, to contact the man on the card he gave me. I promised him I would.

"After Dorian was really sick and had lost a lot of weight, I called the man and told him Dorian had been gone a lot lately, and wondered if it was due to business. I planted the seed that Dorian might be having an affair, or might even be double-crossing him. I acted so innocent, and so concerned!

"One night, I knew Dorian was at the end. After the boys were asleep, I said we should get him some fresh air, and I told him I had a surprise for him that might make him feel better. He took the bait.

"I led him to the carriage house, and we went inside. He was going fast, I could tell. He asked if I was pregnant, if that was what the surprise was! I laughed in his face, and told him how much I really hated him. The shock did him in. His heart failed, and he died — right there at my feet. I felt nothing but relief! I put his body in a wheelbarrow, and then I buried him in the orchard, along with the other poor souls who had died at the hands of the Edwards'.

"I had heard Dorian and his father alluding to the workers with 'no stamina' and figured they either let them die, or got rid of them somehow. Quite by accident, I had discovered one of the graves one day as I took a walk into the orchard, just to get away from Dorian after he'd ravaged me pretty badly the night before. That's when I knew I could get away with it, and I'll get away with getting rid of you, and Nora, too, just like I've dealt with your kind before. I'll not stand for disloyalty!"

Kate stood and backed towards the door, keeping the gun focused on me. She opened the door, and yelled for Virgil.

Then, my worst fear was realized, as Virgil, and another man, whom I'd never seen before, entered the room and made for the bed. I decided not to make any effort to fight them, and wait for the best opportunity to escape.

Even though I was awake, I was weak, so Virgil hoisted me over his shoulder, and carried me out of the room and down the stairs. I was carried outside, and then taken inside the carriage house and placed in a chair.

The man said to Virgil, "Tie her up and gag her like Kate said, "I'm going to have a smoke."

Virgil considered the command, and hesitated.

"What are you waiting for?" the man yelled. "Hurry it up before your mom comes out here, or you'll be in big trouble!"

"Okay, Sid," Virgil responded, reluctantly.

He tied me up rather clumsily, and then stuck a rag in my mouth. I was glad that they were never Boy Scouts, or

I'd be in serious trouble.

I feigned passing out, hoping they didn't know I hadn't taken the drugs.

Sid said, "This woman is really out of it! Boy, those sleeping powders really work, don't they?"

Virgil simply nodded.

"From the look of her, I don't think we have anything to worry about. We don't need to tape her mouth. Who'd hear her out here anyway?"

The door to the carriage house opened, and Kate walked in. She took my arm and felt my pulse. I relaxed as much as I could, so it wouldn't be elevated.

"She's pretty much out. I think we can leave her here for another couple of hours, until Phillip completes the transaction. Virgil, you stay outside, and keep your eyes open—call me on your cell like I showed you if you hear anything—and I mean *anything*! This woman has been snooping around, I'm sure of it, and she may be tied in with the boy, according to our sources. If she is, there'll be more to follow. I'll figure out what to do with her, after we finish tonight."

A train whistled once, and it sounded much closer now. If a train was being used to bring in domestics, someone was being paid to make the deliveries.

"Sid, go help Phillip with the shipment."

"I'm going, Kate," he said.

❧16❧

The rag in my mouth was making me gag, so I twisted my mouth around, until it fell out onto my lap, and then onto the floor. If someone came in, I would bow my head, to make it appear that it had simply fallen out.

Someone did come in, but it wasn't whom I expected.

Virgil was carrying Teddy in his arms, and petting him gently, to keep him from barking. I brought my head up slowly, and smiled in relief as Virgil came toward me.

I didn't say a word, waiting to see what he was going to do. He placed Teddy on my lap, went around to the back of my chair, and loosened my bonds. After he untied me, he threw the rope into a corner of the room.

"You go away from here," he said. "You take Teddy and go."

I stood up, and clutched Teddy to my chest. "Thank you, Virgil, thank you for helping me. Yes, we'll go. God bless you for saving us!"

Virgil didn't respond to my words—he just turned and walked back into the house, leaving the carriage house door slightly ajar, for our escape.

"Let's go Teddy, before they check on us."

We got outside, and the kitchen door opened! They've seen us, I thought. No, it was only Ambrose being let out for the night. When Ambrose saw Teddy and me walking toward the end of the property, he lumbered over and decided to join us. Had God sent him to accompany us? I didn't wait long enough to find out. I hurried away from the house as quickly as I could.

The ground was still muddy from the last night's rain, and was difficult to walk in. I stayed along the top of the gullies as I ventured into a large olive grove, turning to listen for any signs of being followed. How I wished I had my cell phone—and a jacket!

The sun had set, and a wet fog rolled in, making it difficult to see anything but a few yards ahead of me. Darkness had set in. Where should I go? I remembered the sun setting in the west, and recalled that the Edwards house must have been on the north end of town, a little to the east. The Sander's stables were farther east, and closer to Canyon Grove. How far could I walk? I had no idea, I was never one for the stay-fit enthusiasts, but how I wish I had been at a time like this.

The dogs wagged their tails, as if we were on a lark. Ambrose had definitely decided to join us. I continued walking further into the olive grove, until I could see where it ended. Ambrose started to dig by one of the tree trunks, close to the edge, and Teddy joined in.

"I don't think now is the time for digging, you two. We have to get away from here!"

Teddy pawed at something on the ground. I reached down and picked up, what could only be described as, a human femur. Teddy and Ambrose had uncovered a grave. I was certain that we would be missed by now, and looked around for a possible hiding place.

"Teddy, you and Ambrose must go find help. Do you understand dear doggie? Find help, and bring them back here."

Teddy didn't yip as he normally would have—he sensed it would have given us away, so he only growled a tiny growl and stood at attention for a moment. He turned to Ambrose, and growled the same, tiny growl. Sniffing the air, Teddy led the way, with Ambrose following, making away for a destination he definitely had in mind.

As my eyes grew accustomed to the darkness, I walked along the edge of what must have been the old orchard, and searched the hillsides for a place to hide. Anything would do—a rock, a thicket...a cave!

"Lord, please let this cave be empty!" I prayed, peering inside, and taking off my shoe, ready to defend myself if I had to. There was only silence. Maybe I had arrived at dinnertime, and everyone was out. I ventured inside, feeling my way along the cave wall. I didn't want to go in too far where there would be no light at all, even if it were only moonlight. I sat down and huddled myself together, trying to keep warm.

I had sat on something that was definitely not part of the ground. I reached underneath where I had been sitting, and picked up an object, bringing it close to my face and trying to let the moonlight fall on it so I could see what it was. It was another bone, and it, too, looked human. Did coyotes attack and eat humans, I wondered. I suppose it was possible, but after hearing Kate's ranting to Nora, I could only believe that the orchard and this cave must be the burial sites for the Edwards' victims.

I could only wait and pray. It must have been over an

hour that I had waited, before I heard someone coming. I backed into the cave as far as I could, and hunched over to hide. My blond hair would surely give me away, so I tucked as much of it as I could inside my collar, and closed my eyes. It was all I could do.

Someone yelled, "Check the cave, she's got to be around here somewhere." It was Kate's menacing voice, full of determination to find me. Would I become more bones for these graves? Would anyone ever know what happened to me? At least I knew I would be in heaven soon, with my precious husband, and those who had gone before me....A flashlight shone into the cave. The end had come.

"Come on out of there, Jillian," Kate's harsh voice commanded.

I was exhausted, hungry, and dehydrated, not to mention dirty, and disheveled. "Lord, must I die so dirty?" I prayed. I stood, and walked slowly to my captor. She was waiting at the mouth of the cave, smiling and triumphant. I wondered if Nora was still alive. I prayed that she was.

We started to march back through the olive grove, toward the carriage house—Kate was pushing me, and yelling at me to hurry up. She seemed to delight in making me suffer. I remembered that she had suffered once, and that had ended in death for her tormentor. I wondered if she would ever be punished, for torturing me.

The house came into view, just as several patrol cars roared in, with their red and yellow lights flashing. Kate took one look at the police cars and forced me to turn around, and then made me head up a hill with her to try to escape. I could hear voices yelling as they entered the house, and I hoped they were in time to save Nora.

Kate had a gun, which she poked in my back, ordering me to keep going. I obeyed and trudged forward, wondering how a seventy-year-old woman had such fortitude. But I knew. She was driven by hate, and had a total disregard for human life. She had been hardened by the trafficking of human beings who were unable to defend themselves. Killing me would be easy. She might even enjoy it.

After reaching the top of the hill, Kate sat down, and ordered me to do the same. I was too tired and weak to run, so I sat down beside her.

"I almost got away with it, didn't I?" she began.

"Kate, murderers never really get away with it. Killing someone will follow you to your grave. You've just managed to put a lot of years between you and justice. Even if the law never caught you, you have to answer to God."

"I'm so tired of living in seclusion. I really believed that as long as we stayed to ourselves, we could live in peace."

"It's over now, Kate," I said. "You have to come back down the hill with me now and...."

"I'm not coming with you, Jillian, and you're not going back either."

Kate drew the gun, and pointed it at my heart. I closed my eyes.

A single shot rang out, and I knew I would be in Heaven, immediately.

"Jillian, it's okay," Walter said, as I opened my eyes. "It's okay," he repeated.

I looked, and saw Kate lying prostrate on the ground, a single bullet wound in the middle of her forehead.

Walter helped me to my feet and put his arm around me. "It's over now—you're safe."

As much as I was glad about not being shot and killed, I still felt shaken. I knew that Kate would have killed me, without hesitation.

"Thank you, Lord, for rescuing me," I prayed.

Virgil lumbered up the hill with Teddy in his arms.

Ambrose was right beside him. Virgil fixed his eyes on Kate as he handed Teddy to me. I hugged my precious little dog and kissed him on top of his head, thanking him for bringing help. Virgil walked over to Kate's body and sat down, taking her limp hand in his.

"Mama, you sleep now." Virgil began to weep, as he bent over her lifeless form. Walter started to pull him away.

"Leave him for a moment," I said. "Let him mourn a mother who loved him, and cared for him all of his life. He'll have a hard enough time coping, after she's buried."

"I hope he never knows just how evil she really was."

"You're right—she always had her family in her servitude, which is ironic, since she was in Dorian's servitude before she murdered him. I think that God has finally released this household from the clutches of evil, Walter."

"So she was the one who murdered Dorian!"

"From what she told me at the house, there were others as well. I found the graves in the orchard, and in a cave not far away."

"We'll check those out tomorrow. Right now, we need to get you back down this hill."

I went to where Virgil sat next to Kate.

"Come on Virgil, Nora is waiting for you back at the house. She'll make you some tea, and these nice men will take care of your mama. It's going to be all right, I promise," I said, wondering what would become of him. "Lord, I pray that You will take care of Virgil. He's truly an innocent victim in all of this."

Together, we began to walk back to the house after Walter had spread his jacket over Kate's face. I smiled at Virgil, but he couldn't smile back. It was understandable. With Ambrose at Virgil's side, our sad little group walked back down the hill to the back of the house, where officers were leading Phillip, Grant Hale, and Sid to waiting patrol cars. Their Miranda rights were read to them, and they shot angry glances at Teddy and me as we watched them get into the cars. Four other officers, with a gurney in hand, began walking up the hill to bring Kate's body back.

I thought of how the cycle of evil had started with Uriah, when he treated his workers so unjustly, and then his son, Dorian, had been murdered, and now his grandson would be going to prison for the same kind of crimes he had committed. I think it's what I would call 'poetic justice,' I mused — there's no one to carry on the Edwards name. Or was there?

Teddy 'yipped,' bringing me back to reality, when he heard a man approach us from the rear.

"Hello, Jillian, remember me?"

I turned around to see Rick Turner standing there, reaching for Teddy, who willingly jumped into his arms.

"Rick! How on earth did you find this place?"

"Let's go inside the house, and I'll tell you all about it. But first, I need to help Walter get these people to safety — they've been through quite a lot."

The back door opened, and an officer held it open, as three, disoriented young girls walked out with blankets wrapped around their shoulders. It must have been the 'shipment' planned for the evening. Several more patrol cars drove in, and two police matrons assisted the bewildered victims into the cars. The cars drove off into the night to a safe house, I presumed. Those girls were lucky — I thought of all the ones who had suffered up until now. The sentencing would go hard on Phillip and his cohorts, Walter would see to that. Nora met me inside the kitchen with a hug of gratitude.

"Jillian, they were ready to kill me when the patrol cars arrived. If Teddy hadn't brought Rick when he did…."

"Teddy brought Rick?"

"It's a long story, Jillian, but suffice it to say that if it hadn't been for Teddy and Ambrose, we wouldn't have found you as quickly as we did," Rick said.

"Teddy," I said, squeezing him gently, "You are the best dog in the world."

"Sleuth-dog, don't you mean, Jillian?" Walter added, taking off his hat and sitting down at the table.

"You're right," I agreed, "It took a sleuth to know that Rick was the one to go to for help."

Walter continued, "When Teddy alerted Rick that you were in danger, Rick immediately contacted our office to see if there was a missing person's report filed. My people patched him to me, and we joined forces to find you."

"How did you ever find us?"

"After I got to Rick's ranch, I called Ann and got the coordinates you two wrote down from your ride the other day. There was just enough moonlight for us to see the rock entry to the access road when we got here, so we could find our way in. After we secured the house, Virgil picked Teddy up, and seemed to know where he was headed. Teddy pointed us in your direction, and I arrived just in time to see a woman pointing a gun at your heart. That's when I fired."

I was still shaking when Nora handed me a cup of steaming hot tea. "Thank you Nora. I'm so glad you're still alive. I prayed for God to protect you."

"I was praying, too. When the police arrived, I convinced them that Virgil was an innocent victim in all of this. Thankfully, they believed me, and they let him go."

"You haven't been well, have you Nora?"

"No, I've been sick for a long time. I don't understand what's wrong with me."

"I think I do," I said. "Kate confessed to putting arsenic in her husband's food until he could barely function. I think she's been slowly poisoning you, more than likely to keep you doing her bidding."

"You might be right—she was cruel to everyone except Phillip and Virgil."

"I think we had better go home and get a good night's rest, tomorrow is going to be a busy day for all of us," Walter said, standing, and putting his hat back on his head.

"Nora," I said, "would you and Virgil like to come and stay with us tonight? I'm sure we have room."

Rick spoke up. "I think I'll let Nora go with you, but I'd be more than happy to have Virgil stay with me. He has Ambrose with him you know."

"That's very kind of you, Rick," Walter said. "I'll lock up the house and turn out the lights. I'll be in touch early tomorrow morning, so we can sort this all out. Thanks again for all your help, Rick, Jillian means a lot to me. If you hadn't been there, we might have arrived too late."

"Walter, I'd rather not think about that right now, dear," I interjected, "Let's just make our way home. Nora, do you have everything you need?"

"Oh, I think so. I found your purse," she said, handing it to me.

"Thanks! Come on, Teddy, let's go home."

❧17❧

It was after midnight when we arrived home. Walter had an officer drive my car back, and after Nora and I were safely ensconced in my kitchen, he said goodnight, and left. Cecilia had waited up for us, and after I introduced her to Nora, we showed her to the guestroom next to Luke, and told her that Nurse Turner would be there, if she needed anything before morning.

As much as Cecilia wanted to find out everything that had happened, she realized I needed rest after my ordeal, and ordered me to bed. Teddy would be sleeping next to me tonight, I was sure, so we crawled underneath the covers together, and fell asleep.

When the sunlight began to filter into the room, I opened one eye and looked at the clock. It was 9:45 a.m. already! Teddy stretched out his little legs, and I did some stretching, likewise, to get the blood flowing. I threw on my robe, and looked upstairs to see if Nurse Turner was at her station. Seeing her chair was empty, I assumed I was the last one awake, so I got dressed as fast as I could and started to go into the kitchen to get some coffee.

"Good morning, Jillian," Cecilia said from the living room. "Why don't you come and sit down while I get you your coffee?"

I did as I was told, and entered the room. There sat Nurse Turner, with Luke and Nora.

"I see you've met our guest," I said.

Cecilia came in with my coffee, and handed it to me.

"Yes, Nora was up with the birds this morning, and insisted on helping me with breakfast, but I made her come in here and sit down. I could tell she was in no condition to do chores."

Nora kept staring at Luke. He was growing a little uncomfortable, I could tell.

"Luke, why don't you and Cecilia go and play on the computer while I finish my coffee—Teddy can come with you. I need to talk to Nora for a little while."

Cecilia dutifully obeyed, with complete understanding.

"Sure, Jillian," Luke said, politely, "come on Teddy."

Nurse Turner took the hint, and offered to clean up the kitchen, since Cecilia was taking charge of Luke.

"Walter said he would be stopping by, as soon as he finished his business with the reports from last night."

"Thanks," I said.

Cecilia went upstairs with Luke, carrying Teddy in his arms.

I turned to Nora, who followed them with her eyes.

"I think you recognize the young man, don't you, Nora?"

"How did he get here? I don't understand. They've been searching for him for days!"

"Actually, I think they figured out where he was a few

days ago, and tried to kidnap him back. However, Teddy foiled their attempt when he heard them breaking into my house."

"How did they know he was here?"

"I believe Phillip had a contact in the police department, and found out where he had been taken. When I showed up at Grant Hale's office, looking into their illegal operations, they decided to try to get him back as soon as possible, before I found out anything. I think Grant Hale came to the Edwards house when we were having tea. I couldn't see him from where I was sitting, but I think when he saw me, he alerted Kate, and that's when she decided to drug me. Luke *is* Phillip Edwards' son, isn't he?"

Nora was about to speak, when the doorbell rang. Walter came in, gave me a kiss and a hug, and then came into the living room and wished Nora a good morning.

"How are you ladies doing?" he asked.

"Considering what we went through, I'm just glad to be alive. I'm sure Nora feels the same."

Nora nodded, and smiled a small smile. I knew she was troubled, and hoped she would feel comfortable enough to trust us as friends.

Walter became serious. "Nora, I hope that you'll cooperate with us and tell us all you know about Phillip Edwards. I promise full protection if you will. Will you help us?"

"If I can help put him behind bars so he can never get out, yes. I'll tell you whatever you want to know."

"Thank you."

I put my arms around her, and reassured her that she had friends now. Cecilia came back into the living room when she heard Walter arrive.

"Nurse Turner has challenged Luke to a game. I wished him luck!" she laughed.

"Hello, sweetheart," she said, as Walter gave her a warm hug. "I hope you don't mind my coming down and being a part of this, but I thought it would save you both time if you didn't have to tell me everything all over again."

"If Nora doesn't mind," he said.

"I don't mind, it's just that I have lived so alone for so long, it's taking me awhile to adjust. Please bear with me."

"We understand," I said. "Walter, why don't you begin by telling us what you've been able to find out, while I was out trying to play detective."

"Sure, that's probably a good idea. After we talked to the vet, he admitted selling the microchips to Grant Hale. He said he believed Grant was using them on livestock, for clients, but I don't believe it. We've arrested him on suspicion of being an accomplice in their slavery racket. We then checked out Hale's background, and found he was cited for non-compliance in handling his workers, several times. His agency was the front for Phillip Edwards' business, which Phillip ran from the estate.

"That certainly all fits, doesn't it? What about the car Madison was driving?"

"It was mine," said Nora, quietly.

"I'm sorry, but I don't think it was — it was registered to a...."

"A Laura Engle?" she finished for him.

Walter looked at her in surprise, "How did you know that?"

"Because she *is* Laura Engle," I answered.

Nora bent her head in defeat.

"It's true — I am who you say I am. It was my car. Sid was getting it ready to sell for Phillip — I'm sure that's why it started up, after all these years. Sid bragged to Quentin that he would get a percentage of the sale, which would have been significant. Then, when Quentin and Sid told Phillip what had happened, I could hear him yelling all over the house! He was furious that they left Sean to die."

"Nora," Walter said, "did Phillip kill Quentin? It's all right for you to tell us, remember we'll protect you."

Nora's face was filled with fear.

"Yes," she said, so quietly that she was barely audible. "He took him to the butchery, and killed him. We all heard the terrible beating Phillip gave him—yelling, and cursing him for leaving Sean, and then there was only silence...."

"After Phillip slit his throat," Walter said, his voice filled with revulsion.

"I never saw his body, I didn't want to ever see the bodies...." she said, breaking down, and shaking uncontrollably.

"You've been through a terrible ordeal, Laura. I'm going to have Dr. Peters take a look at you. He has an appointment with Luke, and I'm sure he'd be more than happy to make sure you're all right."

"Thank you, Jillian. I think I'd better lie down upstairs. I don't feel well at all."

"Of course, I'll have Nurse Turner make you comfortable. We'll talk when you feel better."

"I need to make some calls, Jillian," Walter said, "I'll wait down here."

I helped Laura upstairs, and asked Nurse Turner to take care of her. She graciously agreed.

"Poor thing," she said, "She's weak as a kitten. What she needs is rest."

"I'm going to call Dr. Peters right now, and get him to come over. I don't think she's strong enough to leave the house," I said, punching in his number on my phone.

I had to eat something before I did anything else, or I was going to faint! Cecilia said she had saved a breakfast plate for me, so I went downstairs into the kitchen.

Walter came in, and sat down at the table.

"I've been making some calls around the department, and found out that we finally have the snitch who was paid off by Phillip Edwards. He's been under suspicion for over a year, but we now have a witness who overheard him calling about the boy's whereabouts."

"Anyone we know?"

"No, it's a shame. I was told he's been on the force for years." Walter's body language showed disappointment in his fellow officer, and I knew it was disheartening, but he soon regained his composure.

"I have to tell you something else I found out about Nora, or *Laura,* as she turns out."

"I hope it's not criminal."

"Not exactly, it's just that she disappeared in 1993, and hasn't been heard of until now. There's something else. Rick Turner told me last night, that he believed she was the same woman he was almost engaged to, who disappeared."

"Rick Turner said that?"

"He also said he believed she recognized him, too, but since she didn't say anything, he doesn't know if she wants her identity concealed, or not, at least when it comes to him."

"I see his point. He told me that he believed Laura fell in love with another man, and left with him, and that was the reason she seemed to disappear."

"Unless that might be true."

"What do you mean?"

"Well, what if Laura and Phillip were lovers? I think we both believe Luke is Phillip's son, which would mean that...."

"Laura could be Luke's mother," I surmised.

"She could be."

"I don't think he recognizes her yet, and it may be a

shock when he does."

"You mean, *if* he does."

"Walter, what is today? My mind is still a bit foggy."

"It's Friday, why?"

"I think I have a date tonight with Prentice, at seven."

"You're not going to keep it, are you?"

"Under the circumstances, no, but I need to call him and let him know. Would you excuse me for a moment?"

"Sure, I think I'll go and check on Cecilia and Luke."

I told Prentice I had to break our date, and although he sounded disappointed, he said he understood, and then proceeded to tell me about the evening's events.

"It's all over town about that fiasco over in Canyon Grove. It seems every policeman available was called in to bust up the drug gang."

"The drug gang, you say. I'll have to turn on the news!" I said. "Thanks for understanding about tonight, I promise we'll do it soon, if you still want to."

"You know I do, Jillian. I'll call you next week—oh, wait—next weekend is Christmas, I forgot. I'm going skiing with some friends, and we leave on Wednesday. I do apologize."

"There's no need to apologize. I have plenty going on at my house—I can assure you. Merry Christmas, Prentice!"

With Prentice taken care of, I next thought of a plan. First, I would need to go out and do a little shopping.

❧18❧

Shoppers clogged the mall, but after all, it was the weekend before Christmas. I focused on my mission, and after two long hours of making my selections (and standing in lines to pay for them) I headed home.

Teddy yipped as I opened the kitchen door, happy that I had returned. I had bought, among other things, his stocking stuffers, and I believed he sensed there was something in the packages I brought in that were for him.

"You'll just have to wait until Christmas morning to find out what I bought you, Teddy." He acted even more excited, when I confirmed that there *were* presents for him.

"Where is everyone?" I asked him.

As if he understood the question, Teddy scurried into the living room, where Cecilia, Luke, and Laura, were conspiratorially placing Christmas presents under the tree.

"Hi," Cecilia said, placing a large gift wrapped in silver and gold, under the tree. "I see you've been shopping.

Do you need any help wrapping the gifts?"

I smiled, and said these gifts were mostly for Laura.

Laura looked surprised, and asked, "Gifts, for me?"

"Well, I thought these gifts, in particular, might be appreciated, after everything that's happened."

"By the way," Cecilia began, "Dr. Peters stopped by to check on Luke."

Luke spoke quietly, "He said I was doing great, and I should regain all of my memory at the rate I was going, thanks to you, Jillian."

"That's wonderful news, Luke, I'm so happy we got a good report. Laura, did Dr. Peters have a chance to look at you?"

"He examined me, and thought I needed to come in for some lab work, after you told him I might have been poisoned over the years. I plan on going over there Monday morning, before the funeral."

"What funeral is that? "I asked.

Cecilia answered for Laura, "Walter called, and said a funeral had been planned for Kate Edwards, in Canyon Grove. He said Rick is handling the details with the rector over there. It's going to be at eleven."

"We'll talk more about it later. Right now, Laura, why don't we go upstairs, and see if you like what I bought? Would you excuse us?" I said, to Cecilia and Luke.

Laura followed me to her room, and after I dumped the packages out on the bed, I went to the door, and closed it.

"I think you should tell me about you and Rick."

Her face turned a little pink, and her lips opened in feigned protest, but then she sighed, and nodded in agreement that it was time to talk to someone after all these years.

"I met Rick when I worked at a title company, here in Clover Hills. He was getting title to the ranch that his

171

parents had given him, and I was given his case. We fell deeply in love, and after a time, I became pregnant. No one knew I was pregnant, not even my best friend who was my roommate at the time. I never told Rick, because I was afraid he would be too ashamed to marry me. He came from a very religious family. I broke it off, before I started to show, and made him believe I had met someone else. After I ignored his calls, he finally gave up.

"I still loved him, Jillian, and was miserable without him in my life. I finally realized that I had made a horrible mistake by not telling him I was carrying his child, so I changed my mind, and decided I would tell him.

"I was two weeks away from my due date by the time I gathered up enough courage to face him, and one night, I started to drive over to his ranch. It was raining hard, to the point where I couldn't even see where I was going, but I was determined to face him.

"Right before I got to his turnoff, I went into labor, and I lost my courage. I passed his ranch, and kept driving—looking for a house I could run to for help. The rain kept coming down in torrents, and I got lost. I knew I wasn't driving on the road anymore, but I finally saw a light, and headed toward it. When I reached the house, my pains were coming five minutes apart—I could feel the baby coming. I got out of my car, and knocked on the door, hoping someone would hear me.

"Kate answered the door, and I explained my plight. She took me in, told me not to worry, and said she would help me. Sean was born about two hours later, in a little area off the kitchen, where Kate slept sometimes.

"I was lulled into a sense of security, as Kate cared for Sean, and me. I never told her who the father was, only that he lived in Canyon Grove. I never did feel well, after Sean was born. She must have wanted to keep me there, and that's why she may have poisoned me."

"They must have taken your car and parked it in the garage...."

"And left the keys in the ignition—I never did find them again."

"Why didn't you try to leave?"

"I thought about it occasionally, but I didn't feel like I had the strength. Kate told me I could stay, that I would never have to face the world with my shame. She said I could help with the housework, to earn my keep, and that she would say that I was her niece, who had come to live with them."

"That's when she changed your name to *Nora*."

"Yes, she said Phillip would adopt Sean as his own son, since he had no offspring. I would be allowed to help raise him, and see that he was happy. The offer was the answer I was looking for, so I took it."

"Didn't you worry about your disappearing like that?"

"No, I didn't have any family, and my roommate had moved back in with her family because she couldn't afford to live on her own anymore. I had saved enough money to get through the birth, and then quit my job, for personal reasons, I said."

"So except for Rick, you had all your loose ends tied up, so you wouldn't be missed."

"I thought he wouldn't miss me, either."

"And so you disappeared, for seventeen years."

"I didn't think it was a mistake, at the time. Phillip gave Sean all the attention he needed, and saw to it that he was well educated, by home schooling him. There were times when I thought Phillip was overbearing, but I couldn't say anything. I taught him the basics, and Phillip taught him subjects, like business practices and global concepts, trying to posture him to go into his business, one day."

"Laura, did you have any idea what Phillip was doing?"

"Not until he murdered Quentin. I was only allowed to bring them coffee and juice, for breaks in their studies. I had learned to blend in, and tune out. I only cared about getting through my tasks, and seeing Sean, so I could go to bed and sleep, because it was the only time I didn't feel sick."

"You never saw, or heard anything out of the ordinary, before Quentin was killed?"

"I tried pretending everything was all above board, just to keep my sanity, but on occasion, I would wake up and hear cars arriving, and people coming and going. I told myself it was none of my concern, and that everything would be fine, as long as I minded my own business."

"Which you did, until I came to the house that day, am I right?"

"When they drugged you, and locked you in that room, I knew they were all rotten. I decided I couldn't let Sean become like them, even if it meant my death. That's why I tried to help you."

"If you hadn't, Kate wouldn't have tied you up like she did, and when the police arrived, you might have been arrested, instead of saving Virgil."

"What's going to happen to him, Jillian?"

"We'll find a way to help him—I've already prayed for the Lord to help us. Right now, my dear, I want you to try on the clothes I bought you, and fix your face with this makeup. I think beneath that frumpy appearance of yours, there is an attractive young lady, who might still have a chance to make things right, with a nice, lonely, bachelor."

Laura hugged me, and smiled. I helped her try on the outfits I had purchased, and after she put on some makeup, she was very pleased with the way she looked.

"Even if Rick doesn't want me after all of this, I know

I'll feel better, and I think he will, too, if I tell him the truth."

"That's a good attitude to take, Laura. By the way, did you know that Amanda is Rick's sister?"

"I never met any of his family, but I wondered. I think I'll tell her who I am. It might be a good start, for the truth."

"Good for you, shall we go downstairs now?"

"Yes, I'm ready."

We went into the living room, where Luke and Cecilia were playing Chinese checkers in front of the fire.

"He's beating me, I don't know why I even play with him!" she kidded. Luke looked at Laura when she entered the room.

"Hello, Nora," he said, casually.

I looked at Laura, and she looked at me with the same thought. He recognizes Nora!

Laura responded carefully, "Hello, Sean. Merry Christmas."

Luke looked up slowly, first to me, and then to Laura.

"That's right—I'm Sean, Sean Edwards. I remember who I am now. And you're my friend Nora, who works for my father and my grandma, aren't you?"

"Yes, I am. I'm so glad you're all right. Everyone has been so worried about finding you," she said.

"Really, then why did Quentin and Sid leave me to die? Why?"

"I can't explain everything to you, Sean, but please try to understand. All that matters now, is that you're safe, and I'm here to take care of you."

"Where's my father, where's Grandma, why haven't they come for me?"

"Sean," I said, "please sit down on the couch with me."

"All right," he said, and did as I had asked.

"Something bad has happened to them, hasn't it, Jillian? I can tell by your face."

Laura sat in the chair next to us, and bent down her head.

"Luke, or Sean, as we know now, Phillip Edwards has been arrested, and taken to jail for breaking the law."

"My father, why, what did he do?"

"We'll talk about that later. Your grandma died when he was being arrested."

"Grandma is dead? No, she can't be… she can't be, she was fine when I left, when I…."

"What is it, what do you remember?" I asked.

"I know why I left the house with Madison, now. She said if we didn't leave now, we might never have another chance. She was terrified of something. She asked me to trust her, and I did."

I touched his hand, "And if you hadn't, you would have had your life ruined. She saved your life, Sean. It was a selfless act on her part."

"I think I understand. Grandma was part of whatever my father did, wasn't she?"

"I'm so sorry, Sean."

"Well, now we know the truth. I'm sure you'll want me to leave as soon as possible, since you know who I am now, or I should say *what* I am now.

"Sean, listen…." Laura started to say.

"You'll excuse me while I go to my room," he said. "I really don't feel like being with anyone right now."

Sean went from the room without looking at any of us, and raced upstairs. My heart went out to him, but I knew Laura would have to be the one to tell him who he really was. Nurse Turner started to follow Sean upstairs.

Laura said, "Amanda, wait a moment, please…. I used to know your brother, a long time ago."

Nurse Turner looked at Laura with curiosity.

"Where did you know him from?" she asked,

skeptically.

"I helped him with the title to his ranch when your parents deeded it over to him. It was a long time ago, as I said."

Nurse Turner did not reply, but only looked coldly at Laura.

"Excuse me—I need to see to Luke, I mean *Sean*, before I leave."

"Amanda," I said, "why don't you take off early tonight? I'm sure Sean will be all right until Nurse Evans arrives. You probably have things you need to do to get ready for Christmas."

"Why, thank you ma'am. I do have some last minute shopping to do and Merry Christmas to you. You have been a very considerate employer, I must say. I'll say goodnight then, and I'll see you in the morning. Goodnight, Cecilia."

"Goodnight, Amanda."

Nurse Turner wouldn't even look at Laura.

Laura's face fell at the affront.

Cecilia walked over, and put her hand on Laura's shoulder. "I don't know what's wrong with her," Cecilia said, kindly, "but don't worry; I think things will work out. I'm sure she feels confused by everything that's happened. I know I do. You look lovely in your new clothes, by the way. Are you feeling any better?"

"A little, but I can't help being upset over Sean."

"I know," Cecilia said, supportively, "this past week has not been easy for him, either."

Laura sat still for a moment, and then looked from Cecilia, to me.

"I don't know if it's important, or not, but I remember meeting Madison when she twisted her ankle, and Sean had Vigil bring her into the house. Kate was out at the time, so I wrapped it for her. I think she and Sean continued seeing each other, secretly. Kate got wise, after Sean was gone for longer periods, and guessed he might have a friend. I was surprised to look into the kitchen one day and see Madison sitting at the table, with Kate about to pour her a cup of tea. I don't know why, but when I saw them, I became afraid for Madison. I caught her eye for a moment, and I saw her acknowledge my fear—maybe that's the reason she helped Sean run away. It was instinct."

"I agree," I said. "Some would call it, a gut instinct. Thank you Laura, I hope you'll share that with her parents someday. I think they would be comforted to know their daughter was bravely thinking of Sean's welfare."

"Well, ladies, let's get supper on the table, and then, I think I'm going to bed."

Cecilia agreed. "That's a great idea. I think a good meal will do us all good. Come on Laura—let's give Jillian a hand with supper."

On Sunday, I suggested we all attend church in Canyon Grove, since I missed the last week's services. Everyone was anxious to get out of the house, and although Nurse Turner went to her own church in Clover Hills, Cecilia, Laura, Sean, and I attended The Church of Canyon Grove.

There were a good number of people in attendance, and Father Perkins was very pleased that I came and brought my whole household with me. He introduced himself to everyone, and graciously thanked us for coming. He asked if we were coming to the funeral in the morning, and I assured him we would be attending.

"I'm very happy to hear it," he said, smiling. "I'll see you all tomorrow, then. God bless you."

"Walter insisted on bringing lunch over to the house, Jillian, he was craving Kentucky Fried Chicken. I hope that's all right with everyone. I'm sorry he had to work this morning."

No one refused the fried chicken dinners. We ate in silence, out of respect for Sean losing his family.

"I think we had all better get a good night's sleep tonight," I said. "I, for one, am going to turn in early."

"Can Teddy sleep with me tonight?" Sean asked.

"Of course he can," I said. "Sean, do you remember Ambrose, the giant Mastiff?"

"Is he still at the house, by himself?"

"No, he's with Virgil, and they're staying with a friend of mine. I just wondered if you remembered him. He and Teddy were the ones that rescued me from…."

"Rescued you from who, Jillian?"

"I'm sorry. I only wanted to let you know that Ambrose was okay."

"I'd like to see Virgil, if I can. He was always nice to me. He's not bad like the others, is he, Jillian?"

"No, Sean, he's not bad, but he is sad to lose his mother. I'm sure he'll be at the funeral tomorrow, and I think he'll be glad to see you again. Now, you get a good night's rest, and we'll start fresh tomorrow."

"Jillian, it looks like God answered your prayers that I got my memory back. I just don't feel very happy about it."

"This isn't over yet, Sean. I'm trusting God to make everything work out—we just need to have faith."

"Goodnight, Jillian, I'll see you in the morning. I'm sorry I acted rudely this afternoon."

"It's quite all right. Goodnight, Sean. Goodnight, Teddy."

✍19✍

The morning was gray and foggy, not the best choice of weather for a funeral. Cecilia took Laura for her lab appointment over at Dr. Peters' office, as I finished getting dressed, and making sure Teddy was taken care of. I fed him his turkey and cheese, and then let him run outside in the backyard to make certain the premises were secure. I had to dry him off, once he came back inside, due to all the moisture in the air.

Nurse Turner had been relieved of her duties, as had Nurse Evans, since Sean was deemed fit again. Dr. Peters informed me that Sean would have to be placed in Child Protective Services, since he was under age, and had no parents. Knowing what I knew, I encouraged Dr. Peters to make sure to indicate Laura's blood type on the report. He caught my meaning, and assured me that he would take care of it.

Cecilia agreed to stay at home and watch Teddy for me,

since it would give her a chance to work on her story for her paper. As promised, Walter gave her exclusive rights, as a thank you, for helping me watch over Sean.

There were no services planned, except for the graveside interment. A few souls braved the dampness, and came to see Kate Edwards buried. I nodded to Iris, from the Jazz Café, and saw that Hope and Verity LaBelle were present. Walter arrived, along with Rick Turner and Virgil, who carried a small bouquet of flowers at his side. A few people spoke in hushed tones, as they looked Virgil's way.

Laura looked like a different person with new clothes, and wearing makeup. She was holding Sean's hand when Rick walked up to us.

"Hello, Laura," he said. "I wasn't sure it was really you, that night—I thought I might be dreaming."

Laura smiled, and gave Virgil a warm hug. Virgil hugged Sean, and told him he was happy to see him.

"Rick," Laura said, "I'd like for you to meet Sean, my *son*. Sean, this is Rick Turner, a very old acquaintance of mine."

Sean was staring at Laura, not really knowing what to think. He shook Rick's hand, and said, "It's a pleasure to meet you, sir."

"I think Father Perkins wants to get started," I said, ushering everyone closer to the gravesite.

The eulogy included memories of Kate as a good mother, and a homemaker. Nothing was mentioned about Dorian Edwards, or Phillip Edwards, or the manner in which Kate died. The casket was closed, because the bullet hole in her head was too horrific to look at. Virgil lovingly placed the small bouquet of flowers on top of her casket. Father Perkins signaled the bearers to lower it into the ground, gently tossing in a handful of ceremonial earth.

One by one, the few mourners went to Virgil and

conveyed their sympathies. These good townspeople supported each other, during the good times, and the bad.

Hope LaBelle and her sister Verity came up to us after offering their sympathies to Virgil.

"I wonder what will become of the Edwards Mansion, now that no one will live there," Hope said. "The land belongs to the family, but who knows what the courts will decide?"

Rick spoke, "I'm sure a probate judge will decide what will happen to it, but I would imagine that Virgil will be amply provided for. The important thing now is making sure Virgil has a place to go."

"And Ambrose, too," Virgil interjected.

"And Ambrose, too," he laughed.

I turned to Hope. "By the way, I think I know what the 'C' stood for in Uriah's log entry, remember?"

"Of course, it was 'DSPDC' wasn't it?"

"The 'C' stood for *cave*. We'll talk more about it later," I whispered.

Rick hadn't taken his eyes off Laura since he had arrived.

"Laura, my mother has a very good friend who owns a school for special people, like Virgil. It's a home, *and* a school. I've spoken to her about it, and I'm taking Virgil for a visit after the funeral. Would you care to go with us, for moral support?"

Laura blushed.

"I would love to come with you. Sean, would you like to come with us, or go home with Jillian? It's up to you."

I held a neutral expression on my face while he decided.

"I think I'd like to come with you and Rick, Laura."

"We'll get some lunch before we go. How does that sound, Sean?"

"Sounds great, I'm always hungry." Sean looked at

Rick, and squinted up his eyes. "There's just one other thing, what will happen to Ambrose? He and Virgil are pretty close."

"I've already talked to my mom's friend about it, and she thinks Ambrose would make a terrific mascot for their school. If Virgil likes it there, Ambrose will be welcome, too. And guess what, Virgil? I heard they have a garden plot that needs attention. I told them you might be willing to help them with it."

Virgil's face lit up at the mention of a garden, and was now excited to see his new home.

"I'll see you back at the house everyone. Good luck to you Virgil, and thank you again for saving my life," I said.

Virgil smiled and acted a little embarrassed at the special attention, but I knew he appreciated the words. Rick and Laura walked hand in hand to the car, and Sean and Virgil followed behind.

The final days before Christmas raced by, with plans for Walter and Cecilia visiting their parents and friends in Half Moon Bay on Wednesday and Thursday before Christmas Eve, and Laura and Rick told me of plans to be with Rick's parents during the same time. Since Walter and Cecilia had insisted on spending Christmas Eve with me this year, thinking that Sean might still be with us, I had just enough time to plan for a Christmas Eve Dinner over the next few days.

I really had no idea how quickly love could progress, until Rick arrived for Christmas Eve. Laura was radiant in the lovely Christmas dress that Rick had bought her. Sean was nicely dressed as well in a pair of dress jeans and mock-turtleneck sweater. Rick handed me a huge red poinsettia, and gave me a kiss on the cheek.

"You're early," I said, placing the poinsettia next to the fireplace.

"I have some unfinished business I need to discuss with you," he said, seriously.

"I see — what is it?"

"Well," he said, "since you're Sean's appointed guardian, I needed to ask you, if you wouldn't mind if I adopted him...as my son."

Words failed me. It's what I wanted, but I now knew that Sean would have to leave me. It was bittersweet.

"I *am* happy for you — all three of you; I assume Laura comes with the deal, too."

"We were married by Father Perkins this morning," Rick confessed.

"I got to be there," put in Sean, "it was like becoming a real family, all at once!"

We all laughed and hugged each other, with a few tears shed by Laura and me.

"Rick, I need to speak to you in private," I said, quietly. "Call it advice for the newlyweds, if you like."

"Sure, Jillian. Laura, will you and Sean excuse me for just a minute?"

We stepped out of the room, and after we were out of earshot, I paused and spoke:

"I think that the blood test you took before you were married will confirm that Sean is really your son. He has a very rare blood type of AB positive. Whether you want him to know or not, will be up to you."

"I see," Rick pondered. "I'll talk it over with Laura, and get some counseling from Father Perkins, before I decide to tell him. But I think he should know the truth."

"I agree, perhaps in time. Right now, what he needs is lots of love, and some time, to fully get over all that's happened to him. Shall we return to your family?"

Laura and Sean were talking on the sofa when we re-entered the living room. Rick sat down between them and put his arms around them both, giving them a hug.

Walter and Cecilia arrived bearing gifts, and we were all jubilant, celebrating not only the marriage and adoption of Sean, but joyously celebrating the birth of Christ.

There were more presents under my tree that Christmas than I've ever had, and it was fun watching everyone open their gifts, especially Sean when he opened the I-Phone from his father. I served a traditional Christmas turkey dinner with all the trimmings, including my famous Chocolate Cream Pie for dessert. The evening ended, and my guests went home. It was now just Teddy and I.

"Well, I'll do the dishes tomorrow since I have all day. Teddy, we need to get to bed if Santa is going to fill your stocking."

Teddy yipped as if to say, "I hope he brings me lots of squeaky toys and rawhide bones!"

I placed him on his towel at the foot of my bed. After all of the excitement from the evening, we both fell right asleep, and slept soundly through the night.

On Christmas morning, Teddy and I went into the living room and sat by the now bare, tree. I had my cup of coffee ready to enjoy, and set it down on the table next to my recliner before handing Teddy his stocking, and emptying it onto the floor.

Santa had brought two new squeaky toys (one was a tiger with whiskers to chew on, the other, an orange marmalade cat for tug of war), a brand new package of tiny rawhide bones, and a new red and black dog sweater that went with his red, rhinestone-studded leash. Teddy chewed the toys to make them squeak, and then settled down to gnaw a rawhide bone I gave him. I turned on the gas log, and went to sit in my recliner. The house was so quiet and peaceful. I sipped my coffee, and quietly reflected on all that had happened over the past two weeks. I knew that soon it would be time to begin a new year of writing columns and articles, conducting workshops, and attending a conference or two. I was also looking forward to Walter and Cecilia's wedding and the upcoming family reunion in June down in San Diego, which I always looked forward to attending. My life was good — no, better than good — it was blessed. After all, I got what I wanted for Christmas, didn't I? I had wished for Sean to find out who he really was, and he did.

Coming Soon

THE MARK
OF EDEN

A *Jillian Bradley*

Mystery

Nancy Jill Thames

THE MARK OF EDEN

While the newlyweds, Cecilia and Walter Montoya, are on their honeymoon, Cecilia's father disappears. And when two elderly citizens in the area are found dead in their own homes from no apparent cause or motive, the young couple's concern grows. During the autopsies, a curious symbol tattooed on the bodies lead the police to believe there is an underlying conspiracy related to the deaths. When Cecilia's husband, Detective Walter Montoya, Jr., returns home and tries to take the case, he is denied for conflict of interest. But Walter decides to join Chief Frank Viscuglia incognito, and enlists the help of their longtime friend, Jillian Bradley, to find Cecilia's father. With her keen insight, tenacity, and instincts from her faithful companion and sleuth-dog, Teddy, Jillian joins in with the victims' friends' and families' determination to uncover the bizarre plot, which threatens the lives of the vulnerable.

ABOUT THE AUTHOR

Nancy Jill Thames (b.1947-) enjoys garden clubs, formal tea parties, and visits to exclusive hotels and resorts. As a lifelong devotee of murder mystery writer, Agatha Christie, Nancy Jill is familiar with life's darker side as well. She now writes a series of mystery novels based on her life's experiences, offering up a unique combination of gentility and mayhem. She holds a Bachelor's Degree in Music from the University of Texas at Austin, and lives in Leander, Texas.

Made in the USA
Lexington, KY
31 May 2011